Yuriarna slowly stood and gazed out the large glass window overlooking the garden. Several rays of sunshine managed to pierce through the dark grey clouds that covered the sky.

"A storm is brewing..."

Yuriarna

SKELETON
KNIGHT IN
ANOTHER WORLD

II

written by **Ennki Hakari**

Characters

Chiyome

Goemon

Ponta

Ariane

Arc

BATH
TiME!

SKELETON KNIGHT IN ANOTHER WORLD

II

written by
Ennki Hakari

illustrated by
KeG

Seven Seas

Seven Seas Entertainment

SKELETON KNIGHT IN ANOTHER WORLD VOL. 2

© 2015 Ennki Hakari
Illustrations by KeG

First published in Japan in 2015 by OVERLAP Inc., Ltd., Tokyo.
English translation rights arranged with OVERLAP Inc., Ltd., Tokyo.

Seven Seas press and purchase enquiries can be sent to
Marketing Manager Lianne Sentar at press@gomanga.com.
Information requiring the distribution and purchase of
digital editions is available from Digital Manager CK Russell
at digital@gomanga.com.

Follow Seven Seas Entertainment online at
sevenseasentertainment.com.

TRANSLATION: Jason Muell
ADAPTATION: Peter Adrian Behravesh
COVER DESIGN: KC Fabellon
INTERIOR LAYOUT & DESIGN: Clay Gardner
PROOFREADER: Dayna Abel
LIGHT NOVEL EDITOR: Nibedita Sen
MANAGING EDITOR: Julie Davis
EDITOR-IN-CHIEF: Adam Arnold
PUBLISHER: Jason DeAngelis

ISBN: 978-1-64275-129-1
Printed in Canada
First Printing: September 2019
10 9 8 7 6 5 4 3 2 1

SKELETON KNIGHT IN ANOTHER WORLD

II

❧ CONTENTS ❧

Dragon Wonder

Furyu Mountains

Rata

Luvierte

Lalatoya

Diento

Maple

Calcut Mountains

Great Canada
Forest

Great Servant Lake

Olav

Selst

Dartu

Sagune River

Houvan

Anetto Mountains

Saskatoon

Telnassos
Mountains

Tiocera

Limbult

Librout River

Port Aldoria

Lydel River

Landfrea

World Map

Holy Revlon
Empire

Great Revlon
Empire

Rhoden
Kingdom

Great
Canada
Forest

Nohzan
Kingdom

Dukedom of Limbult

Map

Prologue

THE RHODEN KINGDOM was the third most powerful country on the northern continent.

Past its northern border stood the East and West Revlon Empires, and to the west stretched the coastline that ran down to the port of Bulgoh. The South Central Sea lay to the south, and to the east was the independent Grand Duchy of Limbult and the expansive Canada woods, where the elves lived. This position afforded them protection from most external enemies.

The northern border linked the Rhoden Kingdom to both Revlon empires—the Holy East Revlon Empire and the Great West Revlon Empire. Prior to the split they had been one massive empire, though they were currently embattled over control of the continent. Both sides were nearly equally matched, so pulling Rhoden into the battle would greatly tilt the needle in favor of whichever combatant they sided with. Discussions on the impact of the great struggle to the north were common behind closed doors within Rhoden.

The Holy East Revlon Empire sought support from Rhoden to gain access to the West's ports and vast plains, which could be used year-round, thanks to the warmer temperatures. Meanwhile, the Great West Revlon Empire asserted that it was the rightful successor to the unified Revlon Empire and was working behind the scenes with Rhoden to suppress the East.

This was further complicated by the conflict over who would be the next heir to the Rhoden Kingdom. Prince Sekt was supported by the Great West Revlon Empire, while Prince Dakares had the support of the Holy East Revlon Empire.

Princess Yuriarna, the third contender for the throne, presented yet another challenge: She insisted on maintaining distance from both the East and West empires while strengthening relations with Rhoden's neighbors, the Grand Duchy of Limbult and Nohzan Kingdom, and also improving communications with the Canada forest.

While these three royals and their respective factions battled it out behind the scenes, the funds that Prince Sekt had been secretly accumulating to finance his plans were stolen by an unknown party, shaking the power balance throughout the kingdom.

The capital of Rhoden was bordered to the north by the Calcut mountain range and the expansive fields that opened at the bases of the mountains. To the east meandered the massive Lydel River, which bordered the Furyu Mountains and supplied the capital's waterways and moats with water. The river continued on to the south, where it emptied out into the South Central Sea.

Deep within the castle in the royal capital of Olav, a man sat low in a well-cushioned seat in a dimly lit room.

The well-dressed man's name was Sekt Rondahl Karlon Rhoden Sahdiay—the first prince. He was a tall man with a charming face and meticulously maintained light brown hair. With his elbows delicately balanced on the armrests of his chair and a quiet, gentle smile plastered to his face, he fit the public image of a prince perfectly. However, his narrowed blue eyes betrayed a cunning fire within, chilling any warmth his smile might have offered.

A man in his forties with thinning black hair sat across from the prince. He wore a friendly smile on his otherwise severe face. This man's name was Duke Coraio du Brutios, one of Rhoden's seven dukes and a firm supporter of Prince Sekt's succession efforts.

Sekt slowly opened his mouth to speak, his blue eyes fixed intently on the duke. "My sister will soon be slipping past Houvan on her way to Limbult. I'd like you to arrange for Kaecks to take care of this. Be sure to bring the priest's mages in addition to the forces we have lurking in Houvan. Once the dust has settled, our people in the church will take care of the priest and his people."

Coraio simply bowed his head in acknowledgement of the prince's orders, seemingly unfazed by what he had just heard. He then tilted his head back up to speak to the prince. "I'm honored to entrust my son with such an important duty. However, if we make use of our people inside Houvan, there will certainly be casualties. And it may also disrupt our plans for the town."

Sekt's smile widened in response. "The Houvan plot is already behind schedule. We must provide our support while making it appear as though this uprising is being led by the people. If we can take out my sister, then any delay in our plans will no longer be important."

Coraio bowed his head again, affirming his agreement. "Understood. I shall tell Kaecks to move on Houvan."

Prince Sekt smiled contentedly and, with a nod, sent Coraio on his way.

Elsewhere in the royal palace, not far from where this sinister conversation was taking place, a noblewoman sat at a table overlooking an interior garden. Behind her, a chambermaid gestured toward the two guests in the room.

The young noblewoman in a simple, refined gown was named Yuriarna Merol Melissa Rhoden Olav—the second princess of Rhoden. Her long golden locks curled at the tips and perfectly accented her pale face and friendly hazel eyes. However, anyone who ended up on the receiving end of her gaze could see the strong will lurking deep within.

"I hear tell that Dakares and Sekt are both moving on Houvan, under the guise of attending an evening ball and inspecting the royal lands."

The middle-aged man sitting across from the princess nodded deeply in response to her remark. He was well-built, dressed in the uniform of a lieutenant general, and wore his brown hair and mustache short. The harsh lines of his face lent him a rather intimidating air.

His name was Carlton du Frivtran, a member of the Frivtran family and lieutenant general of the Third Royal Army. He was also the only duke who supported Princess Yuriarna's bid for the throne.

"I sense something insidious lurking behind this Houvan inspection. There's talk that a member of the royal court orchestrated the previous incident. And a few are even going so far as to say that Sekt's supporters, with our help, made it look like it was an elven attack."

The "previous incident" Carlton referred to was the assassination of Marquis du Diento, one of the second prince's supporters. Yuriarna had been secretly conducting an investigation into the behavior of the marquis, under the suspicion that he was enslaving and selling elves in violation of Rhoden law.

The initial witness statements mentioned seeing elves, though the witnesses disappeared shortly thereafter. There were now multiple theories running around concerning the perpetrators' true identities. Not only were the bad actors still free, but their goals were unclear, leading to wild speculation.

"It'd be one thing if the slave markets were all hit at once, but the fact that Marquis du Diento's money slipped away has only powered the rumor mill." Yuriarna heaved her shoulders as she let out a heavy sigh.

The young man sitting next to Lieutenant General Carlton spoke up next. "Apparently, a portion of the funds was discovered within the Diento domain. A few peasants were in possession of some expensive furnishings, which they claim had been lying around. Other sundries were being sold around town. The Diento family is attempting to recover their property, but that's no easy task now that it's been put on the black market."

The young man was dressed in a simpler version of the military uniform worn by the lieutenant general. He looked similar to Carlton, though thinner. His name was Rendol du Frivtran, and he was the lieutenant general's eldest son and commanding officer of one of the army's largest battalions.

"In any case, it will be some time before the marquis' family will be able to regain their status. It's also likely that Dakares and his clique will take action in response to their massive loss of funding. And I hear that Sekt's camp and Duke Brutios have some nefarious plans in the works." The lieutenant general stroked his well-groomed beard and furrowed his brow as he discussed the movements of the two opposing factions.

Yuriarna nodded deeply before rising from her seat and striding to the large window to look out over the garden. Spots of blue shone through the blanket of dark gray clouds.

"A tempest approaches. Let's accelerate the visit to Limbult. Ferna will accompany me."

She turned her gaze toward the back of the room where Ferna, her lifelong chambermaid, smiled gently, her eyes closing ever so slightly as she bowed in acknowledgement.

Her perfectly arranged hair bobbed with the movement of her head. "Of course, Miss Yuriarna."

"If we limit your contingent of guards to fifty, I believe you could reach Limbult within five days. I will assign you our best men and put Rendol in command."

The lieutenant general slapped his son on the shoulder. Rendol, who had been distracted by Ferna's appearance, stood up quickly from his seat and knelt in front of the princess.

"I will ensure your safety with my very life, Your Highness!"

"Thank you, Rendol. I have heard talk that the Hilk priests are acting suspiciously, so please be discreet in your preparations."

The two men bowed their heads at the princess' command.

CHAPTER 1
To the Village of Elves

I WALKED SLOWLY through the dim forest, careful to keep my feet from catching on the web of roots snaking away from the massive trees. I caught small glimpses of the eastern sky through breaks in the leaves. The day was already starting to brighten, though only a few of the sun's rays pierced the dense foliage to reach the forest floor. The jangle of three coin-filled bags on my back mingled with the gentle sounds of the wind stirring the leaves. I was in the middle of the sprawling Canada province, home of the elves in this parallel world I found myself in.

After falling asleep one night while in the middle of a game session, I'd woken up here as my in-game character. I'd wandered around aimlessly for some time before I somehow ended up helping the elves.

But I didn't have an ounce of regret. I knew any Japanese person would have done the same if they'd witnessed an elf—or any other humanoid species—being eaten, even if it meant offering up a human in their place. That's just who we are...or at least I hope it is.

The tall woman leading the way through the forest was a dark elf, a member of a relatively rare species. She had smooth, amethyst-colored skin and snow-white hair, though her ears weren't as pointy as those of other elves. Her intricately designed robe and leather corset covered up an attractive, curvy figure that drew men's gazes.

Her name was Ariane Glenys Maple, a soldier from the Maple borough in the main city here in the Canada forest province. In addition to being deadly with the thin sword that hung from her waist, she was also skilled in spirit magic, like all other elves.

Her bosom bounced and hips swayed with each step she took, drawing me forward like the Pied Piper of Hamelin. She suddenly stopped and turned, glaring at me with her golden eyes. Apparently, she'd noticed where my own eyes were focused. I averted my gaze, pretending not to see.

I was in this mysterious world in the body of the character I'd been playing in the game before falling asleep at my computer. I was covered from head to toe in a gleaming silver suit of armor decorated with intricate carvings.

It looked like the type of armor that only the knights of legend might wear. Behind me billowed a cape as dark as the night itself, and the inside of it glimmered like stars ripped from a moonlit sky. On my back I wore a large, elaborately decorated round shield, and my massive sword inspired wonder in all who caught sight of it.

Most noteworthy of all, however, was that inside these glamorous trappings, my body was that of a skeleton. Within my helmet a fickle flame flickered—my soul, deep within the skull cavity where my eyes should have been.

In spite of all that, Ariane had still been able to sense where my attention was focused. Women's ability to detect men's creepy behavior truly was amazing.

My meandering train of thought was broken as the two women trailing behind me called out.

"I've used up quite a bit of my magical power. My spirit magic is almost drained. Can you lend me a weapon?"

"I'm tiiiiiired. Let's stop for a bit and take a break."

The two women were dressed in dark gray and black cloaks. Their characteristic pointy ears peeked out from their green-tinged blond hair, though unlike the dark elf Ariane, both were rather pale in appearance.

Sena was slender, with long hair and a piercing gaze. Next to her was Uhna, who had shorter hair and seemed more absentminded than her companion.

Up until just hours ago, these two elven women had been held as slaves within the Diento estate. Since the clothes they'd been wearing during our rescue operation were a little on the skimpy side, Ariane and I had given them our cloaks.

While we were making our escape, we piled the mountains of coins we'd found in Marquis du Diento's chambers into three large bags, which I was holding now. Since my hands were full, the women were charged with protecting the party from any monsters we encountered in the woods.

Ariane looked back over her shoulder. "We'll rest in a few minutes when we reach the banks of the Lydel. After that, we'll follow the river upstream to our destination."

As she spoke, we came upon the path that would lead us to the water. The Lydel itself was quite wide and, thanks to the lack of trees, the area was far brighter than where we'd been.

By now, the sun was shining brightly in the sky, illuminating the trees around us and allowing more light to peek through the dense foliage. I dropped the massive coin-filled sacks and sat down on a large rock. Carrying around such a huge sum of gold had really begun to take its toll. The women wandered around for a bit before finding similar places along the banks to sit and rest.

It was a pretty relaxing spot, actually. I listened to the burble of the river, intermingled with the sounds of the wind rustling the leaves and the occasional bird call. From time to time, I heard the cry of some wild beast or monster deep within the forest, but that didn't detract from the relaxing atmosphere.

Ponta seemed to agree that this place was safe and bounded down from my head to sip from the river before splashing around in the water.

Ponta was a sixty-centimeter-long creature with a face like a fox, though its fluffy, almost dandelion-like tail took up over half its length. A thin membrane stretched between its front and back legs, giving it the appearance of a large Japanese flying squirrel. Except for its white stomach, its entire body was covered in light green fur.

According to the elves, Ponta was a cottontail fox, a rare type of animal known as a spirit creature. They'd also said that spirit creatures generally weren't fond of humans, though I had my doubts, considering how easily Ponta had warmed up to me once I'd offered it some food.

A little farther up the river from where Ponta was playing, several huge dragonflies—around a meter wide and two meters long—frolicked as well, their long tails drooping into the water. These dragonflies would occasionally whip their tails out of the water to toss a fish they'd caught into the air so they could eat it.

In the game, and in real life, these bugs were bigger than anything I'd ever seen.

Ariane took notice of where I was looking. "Outside of mating season, those dragonflies generally won't attack...as long as you don't get too close."

The forest was full of mana energy, which explained the large variety of monsters we'd encountered on our trip so far. My three companions had effortlessly taken care of every threat, though this had used up a lot of Sena's magic.

"Here, Sena, use my sword. I still have a lot of magic power left." Ariane drew the sword from her waist and handed it to Sena.

That reminded me of something, and I started digging through one of the large sacks of coins. Inside, buried among the money, a sword hilt stuck out. I'd found the sword in Marquis du Diento's castle when we'd snuck in to rescue Sena and Uhna. A lion's head was carved into the hilt, its eyes a pair of red jewels. It was a famous blade known as the Sword of the King of Lions. I'd completely forgotten that I'd stuffed it into my bag.

"Miss Ariane, you can use this if you'd like."

Speaking in the best knight voice I could muster from my time role-playing, I offered the Sword of the King of Lions to her. She accepted it, looking the sword over with her golden eyes.

"Are you sure? This is a pretty amazing blade, you know…"

"It was only gathering dust in the Diento estate. Besides, I already have my own sword." I motioned toward the meter-long, double-handed sword that hung from my back. It was a mythical-class weapon known as the Holy Thunder Sword of Caladbolg.

A look of surprise flickered across her face for a moment, though she took the sword from my hand without a word. After giving it a few swings, she nodded to herself and returned the sword to its sheath.

"Thank you, Arc. This will be a great help." Her lips curved up into a smile as she hung the sword from her waist.

"Well, we should probably start making our way upriver. Think you can take care of that, Arc?"

"Of course. I've got the bags, so just grab onto me. I will use my teleportation magic to travel upriver."

I picked up the three large sacks and hefted them over my shoulder. Ponta, noticing that we were about to go, stopped playing at the water's edge and summoned up a gust of wind using spirit magic, easily floating to its usual place atop my helmet.

After making sure that everyone had a hand on me, I looked up the winding river and focused on a point where a rock jutted from the opposite shore.

"Dimensional Step!"

A supplemental skill of the Mage class, this spell allowed me to teleport short distances. An instant later, our surroundings had changed, and we were now standing atop the large rock that I'd been looking at moments ago. The riverbank where we'd been sitting was pretty far downstream from where we stood now.

Uhna, the short-haired elf, glanced around and muttered to herself. "Now that's really handy! Why couldn't we have traveled through the forest like this?"

"The spell is of limited use in crowded areas."

Though the spell was incredibly useful for teleporting around, it was limited by how far you could see. In an overgrown forest where you didn't have a good view of the ground, the risks outweighed its usefulness. You could easily teleport into a swamp, or even off the side of a cliff.

"Huh, I guess that makes sense." Uhna nodded slowly. "Still, it's pretty useful!"

Sena, on the other hand, was concerned about all the magic I must have been expending. "It must take a lot of power to use a spell like that."

Since the base class of Mage also provided supplemental magic, however, it wasn't much of a burden to continuously use the spell. The black cape hanging from my back, the Twilight Cloak, had the bonus effect of restoring magic at regular intervals while equipped, so I never really ran out of power.

The elven women looked at me with great interest as I continued to teleport us upstream.

Eventually, we arrived at a point where the river coming down from the Furyu mountain range off to the north split into two. The Lydel's sister stream was called the Librout. In addition to the sheer width of the river, it also appeared quite deep. Considering the volume and speed of the water rushing past, it seemed like people typically crossed farther upstream.

We'd come here because this location served as a guidepost to the elf village of Lalatoya, and also because this was where we'd agreed to meet the others.

I heard a rustle from within the shadows along the banks of the Lydel. Moments later, several people stepped from the trees.

An elven man draped in a tan-colored cloak kept his

head on a constant pivot as he walked toward us. Four elven girls came running out after him.

This was Danka, the elf who'd accompanied us on our mission into the Diento slave houses, and the girls we'd saved.

The girls were running straight toward me, so I dropped down on one knee to meet them. Ponta hopped from my head and sat back on its haunches in front of me, instantly becoming the center of the elven girls' attention as they let out shrieks of joy.

"Kyiiiiiii!"

The girls passed Ponta around, hugging the animal in turn as Ponta cheerfully swung its cotton-like tail back and forth.

Ponta always got all the attention.

"You were faster than I expected. Wait...you don't actually think you're bringing *him* with us, do you?" Danka's voice dropped as he spoke to Ariane, glancing over to where I knelt.

"He's done a lot for us. There are some...well, things... that I'd like him to discuss with the Lalatoya elder."

Danka closed his eyes for a moment before replying. "Try to avoid causing any trouble for the old man."

Ariane bowed her head slightly, her white hair rippling in the breeze. "I understand." She turned her attention back to me, tapping my shoulder gently. "Well, we can't just sit around here all day. Arc, can you take us across the river?"

I stood up slowly and nodded.

It wasn't much of a river crossing, considering I simply used Dimensional Step to teleport us to the opposite shore. Even though I had to make three trips to ferry everyone across, it didn't take long at all.

The four girls hung from my shoulders as I teleported them across, leading to a flurry of excited cheers. If I wanted to beat Ponta's sheer cuteness, I'd need to play up my wild side.

Once everyone was across safe and sound, we made our way into the forest on the other side.

Even though I was still impeded by the large bags of loot, I had nothing to fear, since all of the elves were able to use their spirit magic, at least to some degree.

Unlike our earlier route, where we simply followed the river, our path now took us on a winding journey through the maze of trees.

Given my terrible sense of direction to begin with, I was quickly and completely turned around, so I simply stayed quiet and followed the elves in front of me. If I lost sight of them, I'd almost certainly never find my way back, but as a last resort, I could always use my long-distance teleportation spell Transport Gate to return to town.

Ponta, however, didn't seem to share my concerns. The cottontail fox busied itself by using its spirit magic to call up gusts of wind, flying high into the air to snack on the fruits and nuts growing in the trees. I patted Ponta gently, causing it to cheerfully flatten its ears against its head.

I was surprised that our party included such young children, but I supposed that was how the elves did things. Even taking small breaks here and there, we were moving through the forest at a rather quick pace.

We reached our destination just as the sky turned a dark shade of crimson, the shadows growing long and bleak.

The forest opened out into a large clearing containing a settlement, though it looked nothing like the human settlements I'd seen. A thirty-meter-tall barrier made out of stacked pieces of lumber, almost like a wall, surrounded the settlement. The wall curved gently around the clearing, wooden pillars standing at various points along the curve. The top of the wall bowed outward in wooden waves, like rat guards on power lines. Farther up the pillars, the greenery increased, giving way to a thorny moss likely meant to catch anyone attempting to climb over. The massive wall gave off an oppressive aura in its superb workmanship and flawless exterior, stretching on as far as the eye could see in either direction.

The entrance consisted of a short, arched doorway,

just wide enough for two people to walk through side by side. The gate itself was made of a shiny black metal, held firmly in place in front of the entrance.

Watchtowers stood above the gate, their gently sloping roofs giving them the appearance of large mushrooms growing from the sides of massive trees.

The girls squealed with joy as soon as the gate came into view and began running toward it. Sena and Uhna both let out sighs, looks of happiness—or maybe even relief—showing on their faces.

"We're finally home!"

"Boy, am I exhausted!"

Two sentries stationed in one of the watchtowers noticed us and began speaking among themselves as they gestured in our direction.

Ariane stood before the gate and called up to them. "Summon the elder at once! It is Ariane Glenys Maple and Danka Niel Maple. We have returned with the captured elves!"

After announcing her name and purpose, she waited silently for a response.

One of the sentries began slowly raising the hunk of metal in front of the entrance, which squeaked as it moved, revealing another gate farther inside. Then this second gate, too, began to rise.

"I'll get permission from the elder. Arc, wait here."

As the sentries stepped outside, Ariane slipped through the gate, followed by Danka, Sena, Uhna, and the young girls.

I watched the elves disappear over the threshold, leaving me alone with the two sentries. One glared at me while the other gawked at Ponta, who was perched on my head.

I walked a short distance away from the gate and set the large sacks of gold on the ground, then sat down next to them to await Ariane's return.

Ponta, however, suddenly had a serious look on its face as it tried to catch its own tail. Round and round, the cottontail fox twisted faster and faster, hoping to claim its prize. It reminded me of the cat I had back home. I wondered if there was something instinctual about the behavior. My mind strayed from one thought to another as I watched Ponta engage in this one-sided struggle.

The sky continued to darken as I waited. I figured about thirty minutes or so had passed.

Above the gates, lanterns of some sort began to emit an orange glow from within the watchtowers, chasing away the darkness. The light seemed almost artificial. It was unlike anything I'd seen in the human towns so far.

Actually, I *had* seen something like this before, back in the Diento estate...

Ariane stepped out of the entrance, her back illuminated by the same glow. "Arc, the village elder has given you permission to enter! Hurry up!"

I stood and hefted the large sacks over my shoulder, making my way toward the gate. Ponta, not wanting to be left behind, bounded after me.

I followed Ariane into the settlement.

The wall was around five meters thick. Though it was undoubtedly an artificial construction, it looked almost like a solid tree. Roots were even growing out from the pillars and into the ground.

After passing through the second gate on the far side of the living wall, we stepped into Lalatoya proper. The village had a rather arcane aura about it.

Inside the walls lay vast fields for farming crops and grazing livestock, the land marked with the occasional wooden structure. In stark contrast to the homes I'd seen in human towns, each of these had the same mushroom roof design. The eaves extended beyond the wooden deck that surrounded each of the buildings. The outer pillars supporting the roofs were carved with unique designs, providing an interesting insight into their culture.

A trail of beautiful stones interrupted this tranquil scene, the path illuminated by torches placed at even intervals along the way. This eliminated any concern I had about getting tripped up while walking in the dark.

The lights seemed to float off into the distance, giving the path a rather mystical appearance under the night sky.

From what I'd seen so far, it seemed like the elves had a much better standard of living than the humans.

As I followed Ariane along the path into the village, we were immediately joined by two soldiers who'd been waiting in side chambers. They kept silent the entire time, likely keeping an eye on me.

After walking a short ways, we arrived at what I assumed was our destination. Directly in front of me stood a massive tree...or rather, a building made out of a tree.

The tree, about as wide as a large house, towered over us. I had no idea how they'd built it, but it looked like some sort of combined natural and artificial creation.

Lanterns flickered from within several windows carved into the massive trunk, looking almost like Christmas lights. The dancing shadows they produced only added to the tree's majestic and mysterious appearance. It looked like a fairy house, the kind you'd read about in a children's book.

"This is the elder's house. Come on."

Ariane opened the large double doors and ushered me inside. Before I even had a chance to enter, Ponta dove through the open door.

What was that delicious smell?

I followed Ponta into the massive tree. Once inside, we found ourselves standing in an entry hall that seemed to run around the outer perimeter of the house. A massive pillar standing in the center went straight up through the ceiling. Stairways marched off to my left and right, and I could see straight up to the second and third floors, multiple doors lining the walls along the way. Several crystals had been placed throughout the interior of the building, casting a soft glow. These were nothing like the oil lamps I'd seen in human towns.

Ariane stepped forward to join the two elves that stood at the center of the hall.

One was a twenty- to thirty-year-old elven man with long, green-tinted blond hair. He had one eyebrow raised as he watched me closely. He wore what I assumed were the robes of a priest, covered with various elven symbols.

The other was a woman—a dark elf like Ariane—with amethyst-colored skin and her white hair tied back in braids. She wore a simple dress, like you might find on a commoner.

The male elf put out his right hand. "I take it that you are the one they call Arc? You've come quite a long way. My name is Dillan Tahg Lalatoya, the elder of this village. I hear you've gone above and beyond to assist my daughter."

The man looked over to Ariane, who seemed to shrink a bit under his gaze.

She'd said that she was affiliated with Maple, but not that she was *born* here.

I took Ariane's father's hand and shook it, then turned my attention to the woman next to him, who offered a gentle smile in return.

"I'm Ariane's mother, Glenys Alna Lalatoya. I'm one hundred years old."

I glanced back at Ariane. She shook her head ever so slightly, appearing somewhat embarrassed at her mother's white lie about her age. In my opinion, once someone lives past a hundred, I don't think a little fib in either direction matters much, even for humans.

I managed to get over my surprise at their introductions and say a few words. "It's a great honor to meet you, Your Greatness. I am the traveling mercenary, Arc."

"Well, we can't just stand around here all night blathering. Would you care to join us for a meal upstairs while we continue this conversation?" Dillan motioned toward the second floor. I nodded and followed him up the stairs.

He led us to a sprawling room that reminded me of a dining hall. It had large wooden tables and chairs, and was filled with a delightful smell wafting over from a kitchen area in the back.

Ponta rushed up onto the table, sitting patiently on its haunches while waiting for us to make our way over. The village elder gestured toward a seat, so I sat, placing my bags at my feet.

Ariane's mother, Glenys, said that she would heat up some stew for us and made her way toward the kitchen. Ariane took a seat across from her father, giving him a slight nod.

"My daughter has filled me in on most of the details of what happened. On behalf of the elven people, I would like to offer you my thanks. Frankly speaking, I was surprised to learn that there was a human out there who could use teleportation magic. I was even more surprised that my daughter was able to make use of this unimaginable power to pull off something as remarkable as toppling the marquis..." Dillan scratched the back of his head and gave a rueful laugh.

Ariane seemed entirely unimpressed with her father's speech and averted her gaze. "I mean, the Rhoden nobility were flagrantly ignoring our treaty. I can hardly imagine they're in any position to complain about being killed!"

"Be that as it may, your actions were rash. The plan was for you to focus on the slave traders, so why were you in the marquis' estate?"

Ariane looked unconvinced even as her father scolded her, but she kept her mouth shut.

I decided to change the topic and brought up the ninja girl that I'd run into.

After quietly listening to my story, Dillan stroked his beard. "That sounds like one of the mountain clans... I think the humans refer to them as beastmen? The humans hunt them and use them as slaves."

Just as I feared, these beastmen were also being persecuted. That cat-eared ninja girl had probably been looking for her comrades.

"This is just a guess, but she could very well be a rescuer, someone dedicated to setting the enslaved mountain people free. I heard they're the descendants of spies who served under the Revlon Empire nearly six hundred years ago. They have a vast information network—unlike us elves, who just keep to ourselves in the forest."

Dillan crossed his arms, looking convinced by his own explanation. A moment later, however, his shoulders slumped.

"If this were a normal operation, we'd send a whispering fowl to notify the central powers of our success. However, considering what's happened, we'll have to explain everything in person at a general meeting of the elders. Using the teleportation point will consume a lot of rune stones..." The elder rubbed his forehead and let out a heavy sigh.

I suddenly remembered something. "In that case, this might help..."

I yanked my personal bag from one of the large gold-filled sacks and pulled out a stone the size of a child's fist, handing it to the village elder. Under the lantern light, the stone gave off a slight purple glow, like an unpolished gemstone.

This was the rune stone from the giant basilisk I'd killed while harvesting herbs near the village of Rata.

Dillan turned the rune stone over in his hand, a look of surprise on his face. "Are you sure about this? A rune stone with this level of purity would provide a considerable amount of power to your magic items."

Rune stones were apparently used as a fuel of sorts for various magical items in this world. Considering I lacked any such items, rune stones were little more than pretty baubles to me. It wasn't a great loss.

"I have no use for rune stones. Also, I found these purchase contracts at the slave trade house."

I reached back into my bag and pulled out seven sheepskin scrolls, tied with twine. I handed them to

Dillan. Setting the rune stone aside, he undid the twine and looked the contracts over.

"The same man, Drassos du Barysimon, is named in five of the seven contracts. I can't say the name sounds familiar. The other two mention a Lundes du Lamburt and Fulish du Houvan. 'Houvan'... I recall hearing of a town with that name, located on the route between the Anetto and Telnassos mountain ranges."

Dillan's face hardened as he looked over the purchase contracts. When he finally lifted his head, a strained smile had appeared on his face.

"Tomorrow, we will make our way to Maple to report on this incident and hand over these contracts. Since we don't have any formal relationships with the Rhoden Kingdom, we may need to send Ariane out again to gather information...and possibly rescue other enslaved elves."

Ariane didn't seem surprised by this announcement. She appeared to have reached the same conclusion on her own.

I decided this was a good opportunity to address another pertinent issue.

"Do you think you could bring this money with you while you're at it?"

Dillan looked at me in surprise. "But...isn't that yours?"

Not only did these sacks contain the proceeds from selling elves into slavery, but carrying them around had gotten to be a huge hassle. I'd already taken my share of the money. Besides, it wasn't like the people we'd taken it from could make any open demands for its return, considering where it had come from. They probably didn't even know who'd stolen it. I said as much to Dillan.

After listening to my argument with his brow furrowed, the village elder finally relented. This was, quite literally, a huge weight off my shoulders.

Even though this world had no credit cards or checks, burdening my travels with heavy sacks wouldn't do me any good, either. The excitement I'd felt while scooping up all of the gold back at the marquis's estate had slowly turned to regret as I trudged through the forests with these massive bags over my shoulder.

Dillan, however, didn't pick up on my ulterior motive and graciously bowed his head with a bright smile on his face.

"Thank you. This money will probably be used to purchase wheat from the Grand Duchy of Limbult, since we have difficulty growing our own in the forests of Canada. Why don't you stay with us for a while? I have the authority to grant you permission to come and go from Lalatoya as you please."

"I'd like that." I shook Dillan's hand.

"Are you all done talking shop? It's about time to eat. To-day's special is white stew!" Ariane's mother bustled in as if she had been waiting for this opening. She neatly arranged steaming bowls on the table, then set down a wicker basket filled with a soft, white bread, followed by plates of salad.

Even Ponta got its own bowl of stew. The fox dove straight in to slurp it up, but quickly cried out from the heat, leaning back on its haunches to give the liquid a chance to cool.

I wavered for a moment as I stared down at the bowl of delicious-looking stew.

Dillan called out to me from across the table. "My daughter already told me about your body. You need not worry about your appearance in front of us." He gestured encouragingly toward me.

I thought about it, then slowly took off my helmet and set it down next to me on the table.

Dillan's and Glenys's eyes went wide. I had to imagine that hearing about it and seeing my face in person were two entirely different things. However, they said nothing, and encouraged me to eat.

It must have taken a lot of nerve to continue on like that while a skeleton with flames burning in its skull sat across from you.

I dipped my spoon into the stew, scooped up a helping of boiled meats and vegetables, and brought it to my mouth. I could feel the buttery texture of the cream and softened meat break apart as they passed down my throat. The bread had a fruity taste to it, nothing like the hard, acidic stuff I was used to eating in the human towns. It reminded me a lot of what I used to eat back home. Ariane's mother was quite the talented cook. It was all I could do to stop myself from shoving everything into my mouth at once.

"I can barely believe my eyes... A skeleton eating food!"

Dillan looked at me intently, stroking his chin as he muttered to himself. I completely agreed with him. I couldn't help but wonder where this fourth-dimensional pocket that was my stomach was located.

"Well, I'm glad you liked it. Don't be shy about having seconds."

"Kyiii!"

Ponta responded to Glenys's offer before I even had a chance. The fox's small portion had cooled, and it had licked the bowl clean. It was time for more.

After emptying the rest of my stew into my fourth-dimensional stomach, I handed my bowl to Glenys. Ariane did the same.

"More, please."

"May I ask for another helping?"

I still *felt* like a human, even though I was trapped in the body of a skeleton. But that feeling became so much stronger when I could just sit and eat like a normal person.

And with that, I closed out my first night in the elven village of Lalatoya.

The next day, shortly after dawn, Ariane accompanied her father to a tree shrine at the center of the village.

The sun hung low in the sky, and last night's chill lingered in the air. The forest was obscured by a light morning mist, making it difficult to see anything but the branches and leaves that spread out before them, lending the scene an otherworldly air.

A small stream ran east to west behind the shrine, splitting the village in half. The forest was quiet, save for the burble of the stream and the soft calls of birds searching for fish.

A waist-high wooden fence surrounded the tree, though it clearly wasn't made to keep anyone out. It seemed to mark the shrine's boundaries.

Two guards stood at attention on either side of the shrine's entrance. One of them, clad in leather armor and wearing a sword at his waist, nodded his head as soon as he noticed Dillan approaching.

"We have been waiting, Elder Dillan. The transportation point to Maple is ready for you."

Dillan thanked the guard and made some small talk before heading into the shrine. Ariane hurried after him, eager to get this over with.

Several men followed Ariane, lugging the bags that Arc had given to the elder the previous day.

Though the inside of the shrine was rather cramped, the entrance hall's vaulted ceilings more than made up for the lack of space. Massive pillars ran along the perimeter of the room to support the roof.

A circular platform jutted from the floor in the center of the tree, illuminated by magically powered crystalline lamps. The base of the platform was covered in intricate symbols that emitted an eerie glow.

This was the transportation shrine for the village of Lalatoya.

The first generation of elders who'd built the Great Canada Forest had placed transportation points leading back to the central hub of Maple in each village. Since then, all the elders over the last eight hundred years had looked over these points. They served a very important function by connecting all of the villages to Maple.

As Dillan approached the transportation point, a small elven man—the caretaker—stepped out of his chambers. He looked no older than forty, although unlike humans, elves rarely aged much beyond that point, even with their four-hundred-year life spans. The caretaker wore a strained expression on his face.

"I've finished making preparations, Elder Dillan. However, we don't have enough *fio* to teleport. So I'd—"

Dillan pulled out the rune stone he had received from Arc and handed it to the caretaker.

"Please use this for the requisite *fio*. I'm sorry for causing you such trouble at the last minute."

The caretaker took the rune stone and bowed his head. Dillan stepped onto the transportation point and beckoned to Ariane.

"We're about to go, Ariane."

The accompanying men dropped the gold-laden sacks onto the transportation point before retreating to the corner of the room.

Ariane hurried to join her father on the platform. As soon as she stood next to him, the symbols at her feet began to glow. The shrine filled with light, and for a moment, Ariane felt as if she was floating. Then the light began to fade, and she found herself in a room that looked almost exactly like the one she had been in moments earlier. However, the platform she found herself on was much larger. This new shrine was exquisitely decorated and had multiple guards patrolling a number of other large platforms, each inscribed with their own symbols.

They were now in the transportation shrine in the forest capital of Maple.

After greeting the caretaker of the Maple shrine and telling him of their business, Dillan and Ariane asked him to arrange for the sacks of gold to be taken to the central council. They exited the shrine and stepped out into the massive city.

Unlike the occasional tree houses built around Lalatoya, here there were rows upon rows of them, massive things with roads winding between. Glimpses of the blue morning sky poked through the leaf cover above, though very little direct sunlight made it through to the ground.

Everywhere Ariane looked, elves bustled about. The market was as active as ever, filled with sellers energetically hawking their wares to customers as they walked past. The sheer level of energy here would put any human town to shame. Though elves were primarily a bartering culture, here in Maple, purchases were typically made with money.

Ariane took a deep breath of the city air and stretched her arms. It had been a while since she was last in the capital.

Maple was a massive city, home to over a hundred thousand elves. Humans would hardly be able to fathom that such a sprawling hub could exist deep within the monster-infested forests of Canada.

In the eight hundred years since Maple had been founded, not a single human had ever been to the city. Even the traders from the Grand Duchy of Limbult, who carried out extensive trading with the elves, had never set foot inside. Only trouble could come from the humans learning of the capital. One of the reasons for this passed right in front of Ariane as she reminisced.

The man crossing her path was covered in muscle, far more than anything you'd see on a dark elf. He had a thick beard that extended past his chin and a slight point to his ears. Though only about 130 centimeters tall, there was no way anyone would mistake him for a child.

The man was a dwarf.

Dwarves had been hunted to extinction by humans due to their peerless skills in metallurgy...or at least, that was what the humans thought. If you knew where to look, you could find them living among the elves.

The great forest capital of Maple was a magical city, built using the elves' spirit magic and the dwarves' crafting skills. The founding elder had created this great city thanks to these abilities.

He then forbade humans from ever being brought into it.

So long as they'd been granted permission from their own elder, all other villagers were allowed to come and go as they pleased. Even in the villages closest to human settlements where trading took place, it was almost unheard of for humans to enter. For those villages farther away, deeper in the forest, it was incredibly rare to even see a human.

Arc being allowed to enter Lalatoya was a remarkable exception, made possible only by Ariane's insistence on his behalf...and the fact that she happened to be the daughter of the village elder.

Having finished soaking up Maple's atmosphere, Ariane hurried to catch up to her beckoning father.

Dillan weaved his way between the tree houses, expertly dodging people as he went.

The two arrived in an open field, at the center of which was a massive tree house—practically a tower—far larger than anything they had encountered on their way here. They had to strain their necks just to see the top.

A small contingent of armed men stood guard at the entrance, constantly watching over those who came and went. Beyond the entrance was a reception counter, where Dillan reported the purpose of their visit. A moment later, an elven woman came out to lead the way to their destination.

Ariane and her father followed the woman to one of the pillar-shaped rooms deep within the building. At its center stood a pedestal with a crystal sphere half-embedded in its surface. The woman touched the sphere, causing it to glow, and the entire room began to silently rise into the air, higher and higher, the entrance falling away below them.

Moments later, the room stopped its upward ascent at a hallway that ran around the inside of the massive tower. The large windows lining the hall offered an excellent view of the city below.

Off to the east, a long lake leading away from the entrance to Maple disappeared over the horizon. The lake stretched both north and south, with no end in sight. The first elder had named this expansive lake the Great Servant. It served as a vital source of water for the city in addition to providing its residents with an abundance of fish.

Ariane and Dillan watched the sunrise reflect off the Great Servant as they made their way down the hallway, eventually arriving at their destination—a pair of brightly colored doors etched with a design resembling twisting ivy.

The attendant opened one of the massive doors and notified the occupants of Dillan and Ariane's arrival before ushering them in. Dillan and Ariane gave a firm nod as they stepped into the room.

It was sparsely decorated, coming off as quite subdued. Eleven people were seated around a large round table at the center of the room, the majority of them elves, along with the occasional dark elf or dwarf.

The men and women seated at the table were the ten high elders who made up the central council that governed not only Maple, but all of the villages in Canada. The chief elder was a third-generation descendant of the great elder, Evanjulin. His name was Briahn Bond Evanjulin Maple, and he appeared to be around forty years old. He wore his green-tinted blond hair long, tied back in an array of colorful ribbons.

"Elder Dillan of Lalatoya." The chief elder's voice carried across the room. "I take it you are here to report on your operation to rescue the enslaved elves? It was hardly necessary for you to come all the way here to speak directly."

Ariane was surprised to see how nervous her normally unflappable father looked as he responded to this inquiry.

However, as the conversation turned to what had happened with the marquis, her face clouded over, and she averted her gaze to the ground.

After Dillan finished with his report, the room fell into a deep silence, the sound of someone shifting in their seat echoing noisily.

Finally, the chief elder spoke. "Well, you rescued the slaves, and even saved two others who had recently gone missing."

Once the silence was broken, a flurry of voices poured forth, as if the floodgates had been opened.

"The problem, however, is what happened with the marquis when you saved those two. It seems rather careless, no?"

"*They* were the ones to break a four-hundred-year-old treaty. In light of that, I hardly believe they're in a position to object."

"Hold up! The marquis' involvement in this slave trading is more than sufficient grounds for war! Did they forget what happened six hundred years ago when they challenged us on the field of battle and the country was ripped in two?"

"To us, six hundred years is our parents' generation. But to humans, it's nothing more than a story. An amiable relationship with the humans is impossible."

"Hmph. Then I suppose they wouldn't mind if we restricted their rune stone supply."

The high elders began shouting in order to be heard over the angry din filling the room.

Dillan and Chief Elder Briahn both sighed deeply as they watched the mayhem unfold.

One of the elders spoke up with a possible resolution. "Why don't we write a letter to the Rhoden Kingdom explaining the situation?"

Another elder, a large dark elf, objected. "We have no need to explain ourselves! If we send a letter, then we're telling them that we were the ones responsible for this attack. We'd be better served by staying silent!" The purple-skinned elder was strong and fit, with a fierce look on his scarred face. Ariane turned to face the man who was trying to protect her. She knew him well.

Fangas Flan Maple was Glenys's father, making him Ariane's grandfather and Dillan's father-in-law. On this council, he represented the dark elves.

One of the other high elders furrowed his brow and made a sarcastic remark.

"You're only saying that to protect your own flesh and blood, the perpetrators of this act. Why, I—"

The man stopped himself mid-sentence as the muscular Fangas shot him a look that could have slain a monster.

Briahn, who had been observing the proceedings as they grew ever more hostile, cleared his throat. "Fangas, this is no place for intimidation, or other such disgraceful behavior."

As if a steam valve had been opened, the slowly building pressure in the room released in an instant. Fangas bowed his head in apology. Though Ariane appreciated her grandfather's attempt to protect her, she once again lowered her gaze in shame at having put him in that position in the first place.

After a moment of silence while Fangas quietly sulked in anger, one of the high elders spoke up again. "What Elder Fangas says is true. We struck a winning blow against those who had violated our treaty in order to kidnap our fellow elves."

The room erupted into boisterous arguments once again, repeating the same opinions as before.

The discussions continued into the afternoon and through a lunch break until a consensus was reached, though it was hardly a productive solution.

"So, for now we'll just...wait and see?" Dillan spoke aloud to himself as he and Ariane descended through the pillar.

There had been precious little contact with the Rhoden Kingdom since the war six hundred years ago.

Duke Ticient had opposed fighting with the elves and broken off from the Rhoden Kingdom in order to create the Grand Duchy of Limbult, which was why the elves now only traded with the people of Limbult.

During the war, the Royal Army and the armies of Rhoden's other nobles had lost over half their forces. They'd been on the verge of total defeat when, luckily for them, the Revlon Empire had broken out into a civil war over the line of succession, causing the empire to split into two. The fierce, constant battles right on their doorstep had forced the Rhoden Kingdom to put off their war with the elves.

Four hundred years ago, Rhoden had offered a formal apology and, as a sign of their sincerity, entered into a treaty forbidding the enslavement of elves.

The prevailing opinion among the current council was that, although the assassination of the marquis might have been excessive, Rhoden was also partly to blame and wasn't in any position to complain. The elders ultimately resolved to prepare in case a formal envoy arrived to inquire about the situation.

"I'm so sorry about what happened, Father." Ariane, who had been silent throughout the entire proceedings, finally spoke up.

She hung her head, still averting her eyes, painfully aware that all of this was due to her actions. Dillan, however, smiled ruefully and brushed back her hair. It was a beautiful shade of white, just like her mother's.

"I understand, Ariane. You're still so young. Besides, this whole issue is far from over, no?"

He pulled the purchase contracts from his coat pocket and offered them to her. During the discussion, Dillan had been instructed to conduct an investigation into the people mentioned on the contracts.

"You've properly apologized, so I'll be asking you to continue your investigation. I'd also like to formally request that Arc join you. He's been such a great help so far." Dillan's shoulders slumped slightly. He looked exhausted. "But enough about business. That meeting took far longer than I anticipated. Unfortunately, we won't have much time to meet with Eevin." Eevin was Dillan's other daughter, Ariane's older sister.

Ariane gave her father a puzzled look. "Is there something you need to talk with her about?"

As she spoke, her sister's determined face came to mind. They hadn't seen each other in some time.

"Ah, I guess she hasn't mentioned it to you. She's getting married next year. I haven't met her fiancé yet, so it still doesn't seem real to me."

Ariane's jaw dropped. "What? No way! My sister, the fierce warrior woman? The same sister who swore she'd never get married?! Do I know the soldier she's getting married to?"

"From what I hear...he's actually a farmer."

Disbelief washed over Ariane's face. Her sister—one of Maple's best soldiers, whose abilities could put even Ariane to shame—was unmatched in her love for combat. Eevin had only ever shown interest in other strong fighters, so the very thought of her falling in love with someone so different left Ariane speechless.

By the time Ariane and Dillan left the central council tree, the bright blue morning sky had been replaced with the darker hues of nightfall. Magically powered lights shone from tree house windows, and the path beneath their feet was illuminated by lanterns overhead.

"It's already rather late. We'll stay in Eevin's quarters for the night and then head home in the morning. You and your sister haven't seen each other in some time, so I'm sure you have a lot to discuss. I have my own questions about this wedding of hers, too..."

Dillan turned to face his daughter, who was still staring straight ahead in shock, and gestured in the direction of Eevin's quarters. Her tree house was only a short distance from the central council's chambers. The two turned a corner and ducked inside.

Unlike the special tree reserved solely for the council's

use, most other houses were split into different floors for each family or individual living there. Shared trees were common living accommodations in Maple.

Ariane and Dillan stepped into the tube-shaped room located in the center of the tree and touched their desired floor on the crystal sphere on the pedestal. Moments later, the floor began to rise, the sound of air slipping through the gaps in the boards nearly imperceptible.

After only a moment, they arrived at their destination. A bell rang as the tube opened out into a hallway. They walked past numerous numbered doors until Dillan stopped in front of one and knocked.

A loud crash resounded from within, then the door swung wide. Dillan slid out of the way, but Ariane, who had been standing directly behind him, found herself on the receiving end of a full-force tackle, knocking both her and her assailant to the ground.

"You're sooo late! I heard my darling little Arin was going to come see me, so I took the whoooole day off to wait for you!"

The woman squeezing Ariane's head into her bosom was none other than Eevin Glenys Maple, her older sister.

Eevin, a dark elf like Ariane, shared her same amethyst-colored skin and golden eyes. She wore her shoulder-length white hair tied back in a ponytail.

Though only slightly taller than Ariane, she was also curvier than her younger sister, a striking figure that would catch anyone's eye.

Eevin stroked her darling little Arin's cheek, almost like she would a beloved pet.

"It's been a while, Eevin."

Ariane offered a gentle smile, but Eevin puffed out her cheeks in response. "Arin, you jerk! I told you to call me *sis*, didn't I?"

Confronted with the pleading, tear-filled, golden eyes of her older sister, Ariane couldn't help but let out a quiet snicker as she hugged her back.

"Fine, fine. Hurry up and let's get inside...sis."

Eevin broke out in a wide smile, satisfied with her sister's response. "Wheeee!"

Ariane had been worried on the way over that her sister might have changed now that she was engaged. Up until now, the only things Eevin had ever shown any interest in were her darling little sister and fighting. But when Ariane saw that she was still the same old Eevin, relief washed over her.

Dillan watched the interaction between his daughters, an amused smile on his face. His shoulders relaxed as he turned to address Eevin. "You haven't changed a bit, have you?"

Eevin looked up, as if just noticing her father's presence. "Oh, Father's here too?"

Dillan sighed deeply and shook his head.

While Eevin cheerfully prepared tea for her guests, Ariane inquired about her marriage plans.

"So, Father says you're getting married. Is that true?" She looked around her sister's room.

"Yup! Oh, little Arin isn't jealous that her big sis is gonna be taken away from her, is she? Teehee!" Eevin smiled devilishly.

"What kind of person is he?"

A soft, gentle look appeared in Eevin's eyes. "Hmm... he's nice, honest to a fault, and a little strange, I guess."

Ariane couldn't help but feeling a little sad to see this new side of her sister—a woman she'd thought would never change. She wondered if she, too, might one day have these same feelings for someone.

"So, you're a little curious, aren't yoooou?"

Ariane scowled at her sister's teasing. "N-not at all."

Eevin gave Ariane a mischievous grin. "Is there anyone you're interested in, Arin?"

For a moment, the face of a skeleton outfitted in majestic armor flashed through Ariane's mind, though she quickly banished the thought with a cough. "No, there's no one like that!"

A light blush rose on Ariane's cheeks, almost as if she were trying to hide the feelings even from herself.

Eevin pulled her sister in close, picking up on the change in Ariane's demeanor. "No, no, no! Big Sis won't allow any guy to take my little sister away from me unless he can prove he's stronger and more trustworthy than I am!"

"W-wait a minute, sis! You plan on keeping me single forever?"

Eevin was one of Maple's soldiers, and ranked among some of the most gifted warriors in all of Canada. If Ariane's possible dating pool was limited only to those who could best her sister, she would never be married.

"It's only natural that someone who wants to take my precious little sister would have to go through me, no?"

"Hey, aren't you the one who just decided to get married without telling anyone?"

"I'm the older sister, so that makes it okay!"

"Hey, that's not fair!"

Dillan sipped his tea and sighed as he watched his two daughters squabble. There was nothing he could do about it, even if he tried.

Slowly but surely, night fell over Maple as the sisters continued to bicker.

The next morning, my ears and nose awoke first to the sounds of birds twittering and the smell of breakfast wafting up from the floor below. I opened my eyes and glanced around the room. Despite the fact that I didn't actually have any eyelids, it felt good to wake up in the morning.

I lifted my head and inspected my surroundings. My gleaming armor, covered in intricate white and azure engravings, sat neatly arranged on the floor next to my bed.

Last night had been the first time I'd taken off my armor and slept under a blanket since arriving in this world. As a skeleton, I didn't think I actually needed a blanket at all, but I felt better having one.

Today, Ariane and Elder Dillan planned to travel to Maple, the capital of Canada, which left me to my own devices here in Lalatoya.

I was overwhelmed with wonder about this elf village—a place humans were rarely ever allowed to set foot in.

I figured I should hurry up and get ready for the day.

As I tried to sit up, I noticed a strange feeling in my chest. Throwing off the blanket and looking down, I found that Ponta had climbed into my bed in the middle of the night and curled up inside my rib cage.

I let out a shrill scream.

"Waugh!"

After delicately removing my dreaming partner from my chest cavity, I set Ponta down on the bed to resume its slumber. The whole notion of a creature being able to climb inside me left me feeling vaguely sick.

I got up from the bed and gently stretched my creaky bones. I couldn't imagine this did much good, considering I didn't have any muscles, but it was a matter of habit.

I put on my armor and helmet. Even though the elder and his family knew my secret, I didn't feel like sharing it with the entire town of Lalatoya. Besides, Dillan had said it would be better to keep the number of people who knew to a minimum.

Outside of Ariane's family, the only others who knew were Sena and Uhna—the two elves we'd saved from Marquis du Diento's estate.

I'd heard that humans were rarely ever allowed into elven villages, so I figured word of my presence had already spread throughout the town. I wanted to avoid any additional trouble if at all possible.

Uhna had already returned the black cloak I'd lent her yesterday, though I couldn't imagine that the impact of a massive knight walking through town would change much, with or without the cloak. I put it back into my bag, ultimately deciding to wear the absolute minimum while I was here in town.

My preparations complete, I was about to leave the room when I found the now-awake Ponta sitting patiently in front of the door, gently wagging its cotton-like tail. Apparently, the fox had also noticed the inviting smells coming from downstairs.

As soon as I cracked the door, Ponta squeezed its head through the gap and slithered out, bounding down the stairs like a newly freed rabbit.

The elves said that spirit animals were able to survive for long periods of time without food, so it was rare for them to eat in front of anyone, at least while they lived in the forest. They only began eating more often when they lived among people. None of this seemed like a problem for Ponta, though. It always had a voracious appetite.

I made my way downstairs to the dining room where we'd eaten dinner last night. There I found Ponta, already lost in its breakfast, and Ariane's mother, Glenys, who cheerfully watched over the creature.

Glenys wore a traditional elven dress, similar to the one she'd had on yesterday, and an apron. She turned to face me.

"Good morning! I hope you slept well. You know, I never imagined that skeletons like you would even sleep!" She broke out into a grin.

It was true that a bleached-white skeleton lying under a blanket probably looked more like a long-forgotten body than anything else. However, saying this to me directly without a second thought spoke volumes about Glenys' character. Her demeanor was much more relaxed than Ariane's.

"You are quite the early riser, ma'am."

"Kyiiii!"

Ponta joined me in offering a greeting to Glenys, raising its face briefly from the bowl to give a shrill cry. Then it promptly went back to eating.

"Please sit down. I'll have your breakfast ready in a moment." Glenys gave Ponta a gentle pat on the head before returning to the kitchen.

"I appreciate your kindness." I glanced around the room, then directed a question toward Glenys' back. "By the way, I haven't seen Master Dillan or Miss Ariane this morning. Have they already left?"

"Yes, they teleported to Maple early this morning." Glenys responded as she walked back out of the kitchen, a food-laden tray in her hands. She set it down on the table and sat across from me.

I placed my helmet beside me, brought my hands together in a quick blessing, and then surveyed the food.

Breakfast consisted of lightly toasted bread covered in

cuts of dried sausage and drenched in a white sauce, along with fried eggs and vegetable soup. The toast made a delightful snapping noise as I bit into it, filling my nose with a pleasant scent. The dried sausage had a unique taste, but the herbs and spices in it created a rather delicious concoction. The thick, white sauce on top summoned up old memories. When I realized what I was tasting, I gasped.

"Is this mayonnaise?"

Glenys cocked her head to the side. "You've heard of it? The very first elder invented it. I didn't think it had spread beyond Limbult and the neighboring human settlements."

Not only was it the same food, but apparently the name was the same as well. I shouldn't have been surprised. Mayonnaise was hardly difficult to make, as long as you knew how. Perhaps the first elder, the one who founded Maple eight hundred years ago, wasn't so different from me. Considering how long elves lived...

"Is the first elder still alive?" I spoke around the fried egg as I stuffed it into my mouth.

"Hahaha! Elves may live for a long time, but not that long. Our average lifespan is around four hundred years."

Still, to live for four hundred years... That was quite impressive, especially since humans in this world were lucky if they lived to be fifty. Though the nobility probably lived longer, thanks to recovery magic and other means.

I wondered if the first elder had been brought to this world the same way I had, but if he was dead, then there was no way for me to confirm this. Better not to waste much time thinking about it.

After I finished breakfast, I planned to take a tour of Lalatoya.

With Elder Dillan's blessing, I'd spend the day wandering around with Glenys serving as my guide...or chaperone, quite possibly. Given the relationship between elves and humans, I wouldn't have been surprised if they wanted to keep an eye on me. It didn't bother me much.

Dillan had said that he still had a few things he wanted to discuss with me, so I figured I should stay within the village limits. Glenys' dinner and breakfast were a delicious extra bonus.

The majority of the food the human peasants ate was only lightly flavored and consisted largely of beans, porridge, and potatoes. Though there was an abundance of meat from beasts and other animals in the meals, there was little in the way of spices. Spices were probably too expensive for most peasants.

Eventually, I planned to start preparing my own meals. More than anything, I wanted my own place, where I could eat good-tasting food; and my own bed, where I could lay my head at night. In the meantime, I hoped to build a good relationship with the elves and secure access to all these delicious spices.

Just as I was about to pop the final bite of dried sausage into my mouth, I caught sight of Ponta out of the corner of my eye. Its head was tracking every movement of my fork, as if connected to the piece of sausage by marionette strings. I offered my fork, and Ponta pounced, gnawing happily on the meat.

From across the table, Glenys watched the scene with a soft smile on her face. A skeleton's face, however, never changes, so I cleared my throat to change the subject.

"Thank you, ma'am. It was delicious."

After I put my helmet back on and stood up, Ponta summoned a magical wind to resume its rightful place on top of my head. We descended to the first floor and left the house.

It had already been quite dark by the time we'd arrived last night, and I only had a vague sense of my surroundings. Now, under the morning sky, I was finally able to see the mysterious mixture of nature and artifice that came together in elven architecture.

Human buildings often had an old European feel to them, while Dillan and Glenys' home looked like something straight out of a storybook, a place where a fairy might live. However, not all of the homes in Lalatoya were built like this. Off in the distance, I could see several more of the same design, but most of the homes resembled wooden mushrooms, unlike anything I'd ever seen the humans living in.

No sooner had I finished taking in the sight of the massive tree house than Glenys—now without her apron—stepped outside. A smile graced her lips as she saw me staring in wonder at the buildings.

"Are these houses much different from where the humans live?"

"Yes. I have absolutely no idea how you were able to construct these."

"We probably wouldn't have been able to do it without our spirit magic." Glenys turned to look back at the tree house.

If each of these buildings had been constructed using spirit magic—at an exorbitant cost, I had to imagine—then it made sense that there were so few.

"From time to time, we are visited by cottontail foxes, like little Ponta, nesting in the hollows of our home. They typically live in groups, and travel along the wind."

Ponta tilted its head to the side curiously as Glenys spoke. Ever since I'd cured its injuries and given it some food, Ponta had been my constant companion. Just the thought of it leaving me for another group made me feel lonely, but there wasn't much I could do. Whatever happened, I intended to let Ponta live as it pleased until the day we finally had to part ways.

I reached up to stroke Ponta's chin.

Glenys offered to give me a tour of the town, so I followed her lead.

As we moved through the streets, the elves we passed shot me odd glances, but I was already used to this from my time in human towns.

The sprawling village of Lalatoya was surrounded by a massive wall. The wave of greenery I'd seen at the top upon entering the village stretched as far as the eye could see. Inside the wall lay vast pastures for grazing animals and a variety of crop fields irrigated with intricate waterways.

My eyes were once again drawn to that strange layer of ivy that topped the walls. It was pockmarked with fruits that looked almost like loofah sponges.

"Madam Glenys, what is that plant up there?"

The loofah-like fruits were semitransparent and full of liquid. Through the center of each one ran a line of seeds that appeared to be growing in the water. They were plump and squishy to the touch, almost like a plastic shopping bag full of water.

"Those are watermelons. The insides are filled with water, but we use them for their skins. After draining the water, we remove the pulp and mix it with herbs and spices before smoking it over a fire."

"Oh, was this used in the dried sausage I ate this morning?"

"That's right! Beast meat often has a rather strong flavor, so we like to make adjustments. Watermelons were another idea of the first elder. Long ago, they were only used to store water."

It sounded like the first elder had been pretty passionate about food. I owed him a debt of gratitude in that regard. If not for him, I wouldn't be able to eat so well here in Lalatoya.

I bowed to an elven man harvesting a row of watermelons and then looked at my surroundings. The majority of elves I could see were tending to the farms, not unlike human villages. However, judging by the sheer number of elves I could see, it would probably be more accurate to call this a town than a village.

"Is this one of the bigger villages? It seems like there are quite a few people living here."

"Due to the...incidents...smaller villages were shut down and absorbed by larger ones for safety purposes. There are about four thousand people living here, I think."

The idea that four thousand people lived this deep in the forest was impressive. While my mind ran through the numbers, a familiar young girl came running up to me. She was one of the girls we'd saved. Her gleaming, green-tinted hair continued to sway adorably even after she stopped moving.

"Heya, Mister Armor, sir! Can I give this to Ponta?"

She showed me a red, apple-like fruit in the palm of her hand.

Ponta picked up the sweet scent and dove down into her hand to give the fruit a sniff.

"I don't mind at all."

The young girl cheerfully thanked me before handing the fruit to Ponta. Ponta spent a moment looking it over, trying to figure out where to start eating.

A young couple who'd been watching from behind with great interest came over and bowed deeply toward me. The man, who appeared to be the girl's father, looked straight at me as he spoke.

"Thank you for saving our daughter. I truly appreciate what you've done for us."

The girl's mother couldn't properly get the words out through all her tears and simply bowed her head several times.

"You need not thank me. I was simply hired by Miss Ariane. I did nothing special."

However, the couple simply shook their heads and

once again offered their thanks. The surrounding farmers began to take notice of the peculiar sight. Later, as we toured the village, the parents of the other girls came out to find us and express their gratitude.

I'd simply performed the job that Ariane had paid me for. Having people come thank me for it gave me goosebumps. Or, I guess a tingle up my spine would be a better way to put it.

After having some treats and playing around a bit, Ponta fell contentedly asleep atop my head, which forced me to walk with perfect posture for the rest of the morning.

We arrived back at the elder's house shortly after noon. Ponta was now off of my head and sleeping soundly in Glenys' arms. Glenys gently stroked the fox's fur as she spoke.

"Hey, Arc, could you do me a little favor?"

"What kind of favor?"

I hesitated at the request, unsure of what she might want from me. Glenys put Ponta down atop a branch in the potted tree next to her before walking into a storage room and returning with two wooden swords. She offered one to me.

I took the sword and looked back at her inquisitively. "What is it that you would like me to help you with?"

Glenys took a defensive stance, then smiled at me and brandished her sword.

"Don't worry. You saw Ariane's swordsmanship, right? Well, I taught her everything she knows. But I'd hate to lose my edge."

With that, she swung. The wooden sword made a sharp snapping sound as it sliced through the air.

This was a far cry from my school days, when the boys would get together on school trips and play around with practice swords. The swiftness and precision of her movements made that evident.

Though I was far from defenseless, I wasn't sure how much I'd be able to help her. She was the master, not me. With a fair bit of uncertainty, I lifted the wooden sword to face her. Glenys offered me another gentle smile.

Before I had the chance to ask her any questions, Glenys launched herself at me.

Thrown off by her sudden movement, I withdrew without thinking, easily sidestepping her opening strike. Without missing a beat, Glenys glided forward and closed the distance between us, striking the inside of my leg and then my side, finally drawing the tip of the wooden sword up to my throat.

"Wha?"

As I stood there, frozen in place, Glenys's golden eyes crinkled in a warm smile.

"You have a good eye, but you react too slowly. Pay attention, and at least *try* to dodge."

I felt a cold chill ripple up my spine. It was all I could do to nod.

She was pretty much spot-on. In spite of my impressive magic and equipment, at the end of the day, I was still just a normal human who'd lived a normal life up until now. When it came to combat, I didn't stand a chance against someone who'd spent their already-long life dedicated to refining their swordsmanship.

"All right, ready yourself. I'm not going to let up, okay?"

Glenys drew away before once again holding her sword at the ready, the smile never leaving her face.

"I'm ready!"

This was terrifying! Until just moments ago, I'd pegged Glenys as a gentle housewife. Now she struck a fearsome figure as she faced off against me. It was the first time I'd truly felt fear since assuming my skeleton form, though I knew the sweat I felt running down my body was imaginary.

However, if I intended to survive in this world, I'd need to learn how to handle a blade. Learning from a skilled swordswoman such as Glenys was an incredible opportunity.

I lifted my wooden sword and locked eyes with my sparring partner.

She immediately closed the distance, as if she had been waiting for me the whole time. I kept my eyes locked on the tip of her sword, doing what I could to dodge her blows. However, I fell for her feint and opened myself up to her.

I wanted to scream, but I needed to focus all of my attention on the task at hand.

By the time we were done with Glenys' so-called favor, the sky was already turning dark.

Though I felt fine physically, I hadn't realized just how mentally draining hours of practice could be.

"By...by the way, ma'am. It's a bit late to be asking this now, but why did you want me to practice with you?" After catching my breath, I finally asked the question that had been bothering me all afternoon.

"Dark elves are known for their physical prowess. Any time I run across someone who seems like they could be a challenge, I want to test their abilities."

Glenys laughed, her voice sounding like a bell. She was a lot more hands-on than she appeared.

"Besides, as a mother, I want to make sure any man hanging around my darling daughter is up to the challenge. Well! I think it's about time to make dinner."

Glenys returned the wooden swords to the storage room and made her way indoors.

As I watched her disappear into the building, I wondered if she'd been speaking to me as a mercenary, or as someone potentially interested in her daughter. I dragged my exhausted body over to the tree where Ponta was sleeping, picked it up, and headed inside.

After dinner, I returned to the room I'd slept in the night before and took off my armor before getting into bed.

Unlike the oil lamps used by the humans, the light from the magical crystals the elves used illuminated the entire room, bathing it in a relaxing glow.

I could already hear Ponta snoring lightly, curled up next to the bed with its large, cottony tail draped up over its face to block the light. It looked content, stuffed from the dinner we'd just eaten.

I waved my hand over the crystal lamp, silently extinguishing the light and bathing the room in darkness.

Once my eyes adjusted, I could still make out shapes around the room, thanks to the light of the moon shining through the window.

I sat on the bed, careful not to wake Ponta, and looked out over the village. The immediate vicinity was pitch black due to all the branches and leaves from the tree house, but this only made the moonlight more comforting.

I looked down at the bones of my arm, stark white under the faint light of the moon.

Was I cursed? Was that what had turned me into this?

If so, I should at least try to remove it, right?

I recalled using Uncurse, a spell belonging to the mid-tier Bishop class that I'd used to remove the mana-eater collars the bandits had put on the captured elves to prevent them from using their magic. Maybe it could also lift the curse on my body.

Holy Purify, a spell belonging to the top-tier Priest class, was also able to remove curses. However, it caused damage to the undead. I wasn't sure if I qualified as undead, but given how I looked, I wasn't eager to take any chances.

It's never an easy decision to use magic on yourself, especially when you don't know the limits of your power. On the other hand, I'd been using teleportation magic all this time without any problems. Even those spells could have had disastrous effects on my flesh...err, *bones*...if I'd made a mistake. What if I'd teleported myself into the middle of a rock?

Still, might as well give it a try.

I brought my right hand over my left and focused on my left index finger.

"Uncurse."

As I quietly invoked the spell, complex magical symbols appeared in the air, forming a glowing, magical pillar that enveloped my fingertip.

Flesh began to appear around the first bony knuckle.

"Wh-whoa! Oh?"

I gasped in surprise. I'd never anticipated it would work this well. But a moment later, my elation was replaced with doubt as the flesh faded from my fingertip, my bleached-white bone once again reflecting the light of the moon. Just like that, it was all over, like it had been a dream.

I decided to expand my area of focus. I invoked Uncurse again, enveloping my entire left forearm in a magical pillar and turning to flesh. My new skin looked almost sunburned in contrast with the white bones of the rest of my arm. I was also far more muscular than I had been before, though that was probably related to my in-game level.

"Huh?"

A strange tingle ran up my arm before the flesh disappeared again, replaced once more with bone.

I rubbed and squeezed my left arm, opening and closing my hand to make sure everything was as it had been.

I tried Uncurse on my left arm several more times, but

it always ended the same way. The strange tingle I felt in my flesh eventually faded as I repeated the test, turning my arm from bone to flesh and back.

At the very least, I now knew that there was, without a doubt, a curse placed on my body. However, even though I could temporarily lift it, the curse returned immediately.

I slumped back on my bed.

My head feel empty...literally. I decided it would be better to get some sleep than let my mind run itself to exhaustion.

I wrapped my body in a blanket to keep Ponta from climbing into my rib cage again and rolled over. I probably looked like some kind of strange mummy.

My mind wandered for a long time before I finally drifted off to sleep.

Elder Dillan and Ariane arrived back from Maple late the following evening.

Ariane wasn't dressed in the leather armor and cloak that she'd worn out into the forest, instead favoring more traditional elven attire consisting of a blouse and cape that exposed her shoulders. Her soft, amethyst skin was on full display.

She shot me a glare, even though I hadn't said anything yet.

Though I would have liked to bask in the excitement

of her new attire, I had other things on my mind.

Dillan told me that we had something to discuss and brought me and Ariane up to the second-floor dining room. Glenys disappeared into the kitchen, humming to herself as she began preparing the evening meal.

Dillan gestured to a chair before sitting across from me, Ariane silently taking a seat next to him.

Ponta hopped up onto my lap, resting its front paws and chin on the edge of the table.

"I've already told Ariane, but we've been ordered by the council of elders to gather information on the names written on these purchase contracts and track down or rescue the other elves who have been sold. However, not only do we have no one to spare for such a mission, but we know almost nothing about the world outside our village. Therefore, I would like to ask you to continue assisting Ariane."

Dillan held my gaze, a grim look on his face.

I was just as much in the dark as they were when it came to the goings-on of humans in this world, but it would also be far easier for me to infiltrate human towns.

Ariane shared her father's serious look. Of course, I was more than willing to help her out.

Sensing my hesitation, Dillan turned the conversation toward compensation.

"We don't have a lot to offer you in return, and the money we do have is mostly what you had brought to us in the first place, so..." Dillan trailed off, smiling ruefully. "What about exchanging information instead? I've heard talk of a spring that can lift curses. It's possible this spring could lift the curse from your body, though I can't make any promises."

"I've never heard of such a spring." Ariane interrupted her father, looking at him inquisitively.

Dillan shrugged his shoulders. "I have it from reliable sources that there's a magical spring near the Lord Crown. However, getting there is a dangerous feat in its own right. There's no assurance you'd even make it there alive."

"The Lord Crown is located farther in, so... No, it's probably not possible." Ariane looked as if she'd been about to say something but then changed her mind

I had to imagine it would be rather problematic for them to bring a human even further into elf territory. I was only here in this village thanks to the elder sitting across from me.

"What is this 'Lord Crown'?" I'd never heard the name before.

Dillan cleared his throat before launching into an explanation.

The Lord Crown was a tree that grew near the home of a powerful dragon known as the Dragon Lord. Having spent so many years in the presence of the Dragon Lord's immensely powerful magic, the tree had been altered. It was now possessed by spirits.

"The spirits lurking within the Lord Crown's bark and leaves have a variety of abilities. The tree's deep roots even have an effect on the surrounding area. I've heard that branches from the Lord Crown sell for a significant amount of money."

Ariane interjected. "However, the effects of the Lord Crown vary due to the numerous spirits that reside within it. What's more, with the Dragon Lord living nearby, no one knows what would happen if you were to anger the spirits."

So, not only was the route quite perilous, but it was no safer once you arrived. Even with all my abilities, I wasn't interested in facing a powerful dragon alone.

Besides, there were still so many things I didn't understand about this body.

I had explained to Ariane and the others before coming to this village that I was a man who'd been turned into a skeleton by a curse. However, that was backstory I'd invented for my character. In reality, this was simply an avatar I'd chosen through the in-game editor.

However, after my little experiment last night, it seemed like my backstory was true in this world. In which case, continuing to help the elves might not be so bad if it led to finding a cure for my curse.

If there was a chance I could turn my body back into flesh and blood, then it was definitely worth a try.

But there was one pressing issue I needed to address first.

"Is it possible to enter the Dragon Lord's domain and come out alive?"

It'd do me no good to venture deep into the forest to lift my curse only to face an opponent I had no hope of beating...and possibly be gobbled up in the process. Though I wasn't sure if a dragon would want to eat a pile of bones like me.

"Oh, don't worry about that. The Dragon Lord probably wouldn't like a human just showing up, but if an elf were to talk with him first, I'm sure he'd give you permission to enter."

Apparently, the Dragon Lord was able to communicate with people. He served as the guardian of all the great forests of Canada. I imagined his abilities were nothing short of impressive.

But when it came to fighting ability, the elves were certainly a force to be reckoned with as well, in spite of their relatively small numbers.

"You have nothing to worry about if I go with you to the spring, Arc," Ariane said.

Dillan, the elder of Lalatoya, regarded me—a human—solemnly. "So, what do you think? Will you continue to lend your incredible strength to the elf cause?"

Ariane leaned forward. "Please, Arc, I'd also like your help."

"I will help your cause."

It wasn't like I had anything else to do. Traveling the world and helping people out wouldn't be too bad. My decision had nothing to do with Ariane...

I couldn't keep lying to myself.

Agreeing to any request a woman made of me would be a bad habit to get into, but I was honestly excited about continuing my travels with Ariane. I might appear to be made of bones, but I was still a man, deep inside.

Though turning back into a human was a daunting prospect.

"I shall join you, Miss Ariane, and lend my assistance."

Dillan bowed his head once and offered me his right hand. "This will be a great help. Elves stick out in human towns. Please, take care of my daughter."

No sooner had we finished shaking hands than Glenys' voice drifted out from the kitchen. "So, are we done with all the formalities? Dinner is ready!" She appeared carrying dishes of food with her, which she set on the table.

Ponta stood on its hind legs and began sniffing around, picking up the scent of the food.

The evening's menu consisted of bread, salad, bean soup, and a main dish that looked suspiciously like a hamburger patty. Glenys had also prepared a plate of cooled meat just for Ponta. Unable to wait, the fox dove straight in, its tail wagging from side to side.

"All right, we'll discuss the details after dinner then." Dillan turned his attention to the food as soon as he finished speaking.

I put my hands together in a quick blessing before removing my helmet.

There was no sauce on the patty, but the meat was so juicy—and slathered in salt and spices—that it hardly needed it. I thought I tasted a hint of nutmeg, which reminded me of the food I'd eaten back in my own world. I hadn't come across any meat spiced with nutmeg in the human towns. I supposed it was another of the many spices available only to elves.

After what ended up being a very nostalgic dinner, Dillan and Ariane shared the details of their plan.

Tomorrow, Ariane and I would embark on a journey to find the missing elves.

CHAPTER 2

In Pursuit of a Princess

I FOLLOWED ARIANE, who was draped in her charcoal coat, as she led the way through the mist-engulfed trees.

I was dressed in travel attire—my full suit of armor and black cloak. A tired Ponta let out a loud yawn as it clung to my helmet to keep from falling off.

We'd left the village of Lalatoya early that morning and were now headed for the Librout River, which ran through the Great Canada Forest.

Last night, we'd decided to start with one of the towns listed on the purchase contracts. After that, we'd travel to the others.

There were three names on the contracts, one of which Dillan recognized: Fulish du Houvan.

He was a noble of note in the town of Houvan, which

was located along the road that connected the Rhoden Kingdom and Grand Duchy of Limbult—the only human domain that the elves had any sort of trade relationship with—so it seemed like the best place to start.

Houvan was a considerable distance from Lalatoya, so we decided to follow the Librout downstream along an oft-traveled trail that would first take us to the elven town of Dartu. From there, we would travel west along the northern side of the Anetto mountain range. Once we were out of the forest, it was only a short distance to the human town of Selst.

On her own, Ariane would have traveled to Dartu using the transportation point located in Lalatoya, but we decided to avoid publicly revealing that a human knew of the elves' secret method of transportation. That information, and the fact that I had teleportation magic of my own, would be best to keep to as few people as possible.

Between Transport Gate, which would teleport me to any location I had previously visited, and Dimensional Step, a spell allowing me to teleport short distances, traveling wasn't much of an issue for me.

However, here in the forest, surrounded by trees and dense undergrowth, I couldn't use Dimensional Step. We had no choice but to walk, hefting our bags along this unmarked path—not that Ponta was actually walking.

Also, according to Ariane, the mist that hung around us inhibited the use of magic. The mist itself wasn't terribly thick. Oddly enough, it looked a lot like the spray of snow thrown up behind a skier. It made objects in the distance a little hazy, but I could still see them well enough. Regardless, when surrounded by this kind of mist, which existed only in forests, valleys, and other places full of mana energy, it had a dulling effect on the user's magic, making it much harder to control—or even unusable. Even simple abilities, like summoning a flame, could be affected in all sorts of unpredictable ways.

However, this effect was typically restricted to humans. The mist had no impact on elves and their control over spirit magic, or on monsters and other spirit animals.

After a while of trudging through the mist-filled forest, we finally heard the sound of rushing water up ahead. We'd made it to our first checkpoint, the Librout River.

The air cleared as soon as we reached the bank. For one reason or another—perhaps the light breeze—the mist was much thinner here. I could see quite far, both up and downstream.

Unfortunately, the clear air brought a new set of issues with it. Up ahead, I could see a group of dragonflies flying along the river.

The insects seemed to view our sudden appearance as a threat. They snapped their mandibles and emitted an ear-splitting shriek as they spread their massive, translucent wings and launched their two-meter-long frames toward us. The sight of them alone would have haunted a person afraid of insects for life.

"Watch out, Arc!"

"Huh?"

Ariane pulled her sword from the sheath at her waist in a well-practiced motion, squaring off against the dragonflies. Every time she swung her blade, it sent her long, white hair fluttering among the severed wings and thoraxes.

I wasn't equipped to deal with multiple dragonflies at once, so I relied on my Dimensional Step. The lack of mist along the riverbank made it easy to put some distance between me and the oncoming threat.

I readied myself for combat.

If Glenys could see me now, she'd probably ask me for the "favor" of another intense training session. The image of her gentle smile and brutal blows comforted me.

I didn't have anything against insects, but these dragonflies reminded me of a traumatic experience I had as a kid, when a cockroach flew right onto my clothes and held tight. At least, that was the excuse I gave myself as

I prepared to face off against the massive creatures, who were now frantically searching for a target that had disappeared in front of their multifaceted eyes.

I drew my sword and charged. The blade gave off a light blue glow as I slashed it sideways, cleaving a dragonfly clean in two. Even after it hit the ground, its wings were still beating in the sand of the riverbank. I crushed its flailing body with my armored boot as I turned to face the other airborne enemies.

The remaining dragonflies quickly realized that this was not a battle they would win. They fled upstream, leaving only the ominous sound of flapping wings in their wake.

A few moments later, we were once again enveloped in the peaceful burble of the flowing river and the gentle rustling of leaves.

Ariane carefully wiped the dragonfly blood from her sword with a cloth before returning it to her sheath.

"It looks like the mist doesn't reach the riverbank, so we should be able to teleport downstream." She sounded slightly winded.

I nodded in agreement. After making sure that Ariane had a firm grip on my shoulder, I used Dimensional Step to teleport down the Librout.

The mist began to burn off as the sun rose in the sky, giving us an even better view.

Around noon, we took a short break at a large rock beside the river and ate the lunch that Glenys had prepared for us. Then, we resumed our trip.

Mountains came into view just as the sun began to set, looming large in the distance. This was the Anetto mountain range I had heard about.

In the forest to the east lay the elven village of Dartu. The village looked almost identical to Lalatoya. However, the walls were surrounded by a massive moat fed by the Librout River, preventing anyone from getting too close. A raised suspension bridge jutted out from the gate. I spotted several of the mushroom-shaped houses I'd seen back in Lalatoya scattered about the open area in front of the moat.

Ariane didn't seem particularly impressed by the scene in front of us. She called to an elf stationed in one of the watchtowers built into the wall.

"I am Ariane Glenys Maple! I am here on a mission, on my way to a human town. I would like to request accommodations for the night!"

The man in the tower glanced in my direction before turning to speak with another guard next to him. After a moment, he responded to Ariane.

"You may enter! The town will provide you with a meal and a hut for the night."

Ariane bowed her head in appreciation, then turned to me. "We'll be spending the night in one of the huts over there. Tomorrow morning, we'll make our way west. Once we're out of the forest, we'll see the Rhoden town of Selst."

"Finally. We've traveled quite a long way already."

"Under normal circumstances, it takes around four days to make it here on foot from Lalatoya." Ariane gave me a surprised look before leading the way to one of the huts.

The flat-roofed, mushroom-shaped building was actually rather spacious inside. It consisted of a stone floor, a fireplace for heating and cooking, and a large pillar in the center of the room. To the left of the pillar were a table and four chairs. To the right, four beds were lined up against the wall under the window. There was no other furniture.

I set my bag next to the central pillar and sat on one of the beds. Ponta hopped down from its perch atop my helmet and walked around the room, tilting its head to the side as it investigated our new surroundings. It left paw prints in the dust with each step.

Apparently, they didn't clean these huts.

I opened the window and shook out the blanket, sending up a massive cloud of dust. Ponta summoned a magical gust of wind—probably to help clear out the room—but this only stirred up more particles.

"I'm going to speak with the Dartu elder. Could you do something about all this dust while I'm gone?" Ariane waved a hand in front of her face as she spoke, trying to stave off a coughing fit with a look of annoyance on her face.

I nodded. "I'll take care of the beds first."

After seeing Ariane off, I took another look around the hut. I grabbed a broom from against the wall next to the fireplace and started sweeping.

After collecting most of the dust, I grabbed a wooden bucket and washcloth from the corner of the room and went outside. The sky had already turned crimson, and the forest was an indistinguishable black mass.

I couldn't find a well anywhere near the cluster of huts, so I made my way to the moat instead. I figured this was probably where people got their water. A stairwell led down to the moat's surface.

I returned to the hut, dumped the washcloth into the bucket, and squeezed out the excess water. Then I wiped down the tables, the chairs, and the rest of the room. Once I was done, the hut actually looked pretty nice.

"Huh, I guess that's about it."

Truth be told, I enjoyed cleaning, laundry, cooking, and other chores. I crossed my arms and looked around the room, satisfied with my work. Then I gathered up the bucket and went outside to dump the dirty water.

As I stepped out of the hut, I spotted Ariane walking across the lowered suspension bridge, holding a covered stewpot and cloth bag. She showed me what she was holding.

"I've brought dinner!"

Arianne's glossy lips curved up into a smile, and her amethyst cheeks took on a light shade of pink. Her long white hair, usually tied back in a ponytail, was slightly damp as it hung loose, blowing gently in the breeze. I caught the scent of flowers from her direction. She had the appearance of a woman freshly out of the bath.

"D-did you just take a bath?" I blurted out without thinking.

Though she was usually rather reserved, her eyes went wide at my reaction. Then she gave a nod. "I did back in Lalatoya, too, you know. I guess humans don't bathe all that often?"

"What? There were baths back in Lalatoya? I wish I'd known..."

Ariane regarded me with confusion as my shoulders slumped.

I hadn't had the chance to bathe *once* since coming to this world. If only I'd known there was a bath in Ariane's house. I was so frustrated at my own inattention, I almost cursed myself. But to be fair, I already was cursed.

"Oh, did you want to take a bath?"

"I did..."

"Why would a skeleton need to wash itself?"

"How rude! I was a compulsively clean person back when I was a human!"

Ariane ignored my outburst and suggested that we eat dinner. Ponta let out a *kyiii* of agreement and ran after her into the hut.

Outnumbered, I followed them inside, scowling the whole way.

The stewpot contained a bean and bacon soup, and the cloth bag held some bread, wooden bowls, and several red fruits.

While Ariane ladled the soup into the bowls, I glanced back around the room again just in case I'd missed something, but I was quickly disappointed.

"There's no bath in here."

Ariane ignored my grumblings and handed some fruit to Ponta.

"These huts were only built for humans who got lost in the woods."

Dartu was located just fifty kilometers east of Selst and thirty kilometers north of the Grand Duchy of Limbult. Humans who strayed from the path to escape monsters often ended up here. These huts provided temporary lodgings for them. That explained why they had only the bare necessities and lacked the magical crystal lamps found in elven homes.

A pathetic flame hovered above the oil lamp atop the table, offering minimal illumination.

The next time we were in Lalatoya, I'd ask to take a bath.

I ate the salty bacon and bean soup in silence, vowing to get my hands on some spices for my future travels.

We left Dartu early the next morning and headed west, the Anetto mountain range our constant companion to the south. Like the day before, we were forced to travel on foot throughout the morning due to all the mist.

We did encounter the occasional monster, which would invariably bare its fangs and attack us, but these distractions only slowed us slightly.

Once the sun was high in the sky and the mist began to clear, we able to start teleporting again. This improved our progress somewhat, though I wasn't able to use my magic to its full potential due to the poor visibility in the forest.

When we finally broke out of the trees and caught sight of the town of Selst, the sun was staring to sink in the western sky.

The town was built in a similar style to Luvierte—the first town I'd visited when I came to this world—in the middle of a vast plain. The crops in the surrounding fields appeared to be primarily vegetables, with little in the way of staple grains. An empty moat and dirt wall faced the forest, in order to ward off the monsters that lurked in the trees.

The two of us—a dark elf in a charcoal cloak who hid her pointed ears and amethyst skin, and a massive knight draped in black—must have been quite the sight as we walked along the road between the fields of Selst.

Farmers stopped their work and turned toward us as we approached the town, but we ignored their stares. Two guards stood watch at the gate. After paying the entrance tax, we entered Selst.

"We should probably look for a place to stay first."

Ariane's response was curt. "Right."

She glanced around, a look of wonder on her face. Night had already fallen when we'd entered Diento, so it was probably strange for her to see a human town in the light of the setting sun.

The streets were packed with people, the air full of the sounds of shops closing up, hawkers calling for last orders, and the general bustle of a town at nightfall. The mass of people parted for me as I walked. Between the black cloak on my back and Ponta atop my head, I must have struck an intimidating figure.

We passed a building with a group of men clad in metal and leather armor milling about out front. The familiar sign indicated that this was the mercenary guild office. The mercenaries crowded around it were carefully checking their weapons and talking among themselves. Mercenaries tended to talk in loud voices, and these were no exception. Each was yelling to be heard over the rest.

I slowed my pace, curious to hear what they were discussing.

"So, how did it go?"

"I didn't find anything."

A massive man sporting an unkempt beard, metal armor, and an oversized shield at his feet was speaking to an attractive young man in front of him. The young man was clad in leather armor and had a bow slung over his back. He shrugged his shoulders in an exaggerated motion and shook his head.

"One of our scouts spotted one, but it got away."

"Ten men in seven days...huh. Doubt they'll show themselves while we're here."

"There are already ten dead? That's quite a bit. Still, we can't do much with our numbers. Setting traps is a waste of time. They're too smart for that."

"If we can't slay the haunted wolves, then it's only a matter of time until the count gets involved."

Ariane's head snapped up, as if she'd heard something important.

Judging by the conversation between the mercenaries, monsters were coming out of the forest at the base of the Anetto Mountains, and the town's mercenary troupe had called an emergency meeting to deal with them.

It looked like the mercenaries had a considerable force. The haunted wolves must have been quite a problem to draw this many men. A call like this typically only included mercenaries who belonged to the town's troupe, but in the event that war broke out with another noble, or even another country, then *all* the mercenaries living here would have to answer an emergency call. As such, it'd probably be a good idea to avoid entering the town under my mercenary license.

Ariane tugged at my cloak. I turned. Ponta looked around curiously, wondering why we'd suddenly stopped.

"Arc, there's something I'd like to discuss once we make it to the inn."

"Understood. Let's hurry up and find a place to stay."

After a cursory search for a sufficient inn, we found ourselves in a relatively clean one operated by an older woman. I reserved two rooms on the second floor and gave one of the keys to Ariane. She took the key, picked up her bags, and made her way upstairs.

After seeing her off, I turned to the innkeeper. "Excuse me, miss, but could you tell me how to get to Houvan from here?"

"Miss? Cut it out, Sir Knight. You're making me blush!"

The woman had a rather hefty frame, which shook as she let out a boisterous laugh. She reminded me of the older women in my neighborhood.

"Houvan, right? Well, you'll want to leave through the south gate and follow the road that runs parallel to the woods. It'll take you around two days by carriage. Skilled fighters apparently cut straight through the woods, but it's probably not a good idea right now."

"Because of the haunted wolves?"

"Right! At least ten people have been eaten over the past few days. Monsters don't usually leave the forest here. Seems like these ones are coming down out of the Anetto Mountains for some reason. It's got the whole town on edge."

The innkeeper shrugged her shoulders and let out a heavy sigh.

She told me that haunted wolves had started appearing along the road, attacking travelers and merchants. As the story spread to neighboring towns, fewer and fewer people came to Selst. The local nobility called the mercenary troupe and ordered them to slay the haunted wolves—not a bad proposition, since they would be able to sell the pelts for a tidy sum. However, they'd seen little success so far.

After listening to her story, I made my way to my room.

I set my bags down, removed my cloak, and sat on the bed. Ponta summoned up a gust of magical wind to fly over to the window and look out at the town below. A moment later, I heard a knock at the door. Ariane announced herself before stepping inside.

As soon as the door was closed, she yanked off her hood, sending her long, white hair spilling down and revealing her amethyst features.

Her usual confidence was missing from her golden eyes, which were downcast. She seemed uncertain about something, so I waited. After a long moment, she finally spoke.

"Arc...I'd like to go to the forests at the base of the mountain tomorrow."

"Hm? I heard it's faster to head southwest and cut through the forest...but I'm guessing that's not what this is about?"

She nodded. "It has to do with the haunted wolves we heard the mercenaries talking about. If possible, I'd like to take a small detour tomorrow to get my hand on a wolf tail."

"Your wish is my command. If it's a wolf tail you need, then I will do my best to assist."

In the face of such an uncommon request—from Ariane of all people, a woman who needed no man's help—how could I say no?

I hoped my eager agreement would please her, though she looked slightly ashamed for having asked this of me.

"Actually, my sister is about to get married."

"Oh, that's fantastic news!"

This conversation seemed to have come out of nowhere, so I simply nodded and prompted her to continue.

"I'd like to give her a veil made from the fur of a haunted wolf's tail."

She looked a bit sad as she spoke, but once she'd finished, she looked back up at me with a smile and explained her plan.

According to Ariane, haunted wolves' tails glowed a deep blue in the presence of abundant mana. Veils made out of their fur gave off a unique light when worn, making them a rather expensive gift.

However, getting a tail was no easy task. Haunted wolves were a difficult beast to hunt, thanks to their ability to create multiple illusions to confuse their prey.

A monster that could summon shadow copies of itself...

Ariane would have no trouble taking a haunted wolf down on its own, but unfortunately, these monsters tended to travel in packs.

She seemed a bit worried about asking me for a favor that had nothing to do with saving her fellow elves. However, I understood. When a rare opportunity crossed your path, it was only natural to want to take it.

What's more, since she was doing this as a gift for her sister, I really had no reason to refuse. My biggest concern was the monsters' strength, but if she was capable of taking one down on her own, then we would be fine...so long as I stayed alert.

"All right, tomorrow we'll head through the forest along the base of the Anetto Mountains on the way to Houvan."

"Thank you, Arc."

With that out of the way, Ariane's cheeks flushed, and she bowed her head.

I could have stared at her embarrassed expression forever, but after only a moment of my gawking, her golden eyes darted back up to mine, glaring.

I cleared my throat. "Shall I go buy us some dinner? And probably some rations for tomorrow, as well."

"Kyiii!"

Ponta cut its yawn short and responded enthusiastically. A gust of magical wind sent it flying over from the window to land on my face. It scurried up to perch on top of my helmet.

As I made stepped out into the town, dyed orange by the setting sun, I wondered just how Ponta was able to understand our conversations.

We left Selst first thing the following morning, heading straight toward the forest facing the southern gate.

The most commonly traveled route ran along the edge of the forest. However, we marched straight into the woods, making our way toward the Telnassos mountain range to the southwest.

Without a compass, it would have been almost impossible for me to find the right direction. But Ariane, true to her elven upbringing, seemed to have no problem.

There was a light haze hanging in the air here as well, but it was nothing like the magic-blocking mist we'd been confronted with in Canada, so I was able to use Dimensional Step. However, the forest grew denser the farther in we traveled, making it difficult to use the teleportation magic to its full effect.

I'd noticed the day before that the forests on this side of the Librout River were notably different from those in Canada. Compared to the massive, ancient hardwoods that made up the elven realm, the trees were far more like what I was accustomed to seeing elsewhere in the world.

Whenever we came to a large enough opening, I used Dimensional Step to speed up our progress.

Around noon, we found a small clearing and sat down to eat the food I'd purchased the day before.

Our lunch consisted of dried potatoes and salted smoked meat, along with some walnuts and dried apples. In total, it had cost a little over three silver coins, though the apples were one silver coin on their own. I still had over a thousand gold coins in my leather purse, though, so I wasn't terribly concerned about money. In fact, I really had no use for it outside of lodgings and food. Spending a little extra on fruit was worth it just to see Ponta's expression as it stared longingly at the dried apples, its tail wagging excitedly.

"You're being so mean!"

I'd been playfully holding a piece of apple just out of the fox's reach when Ariane scolded me. I patted Ponta on the head before giving it the object of its desire.

I summoned up Fire to lightly roast my dried potatoes. However, the flame was too strong, and I wound up turning them into a charred lump.

"You're pretty clumsy, Arc."

Ariane summoned up her spirit magic, perfectly grilling her own potatoes.

I gnawed at my charred mess, newly impressed with

my companion—and newly ashamed at my lack of ability to control my magic. I needed to practice more.

After we finished lunch, Ariane once again led the way into the woods.

Ponta had abandoned its usual perch in favor of sleeping in Ariane's bosom. I was jealous for a multitude of reasons.

I had no idea how deep into the forest we'd traveled at this point, but the bird calls and animal cries had died off, leaving only the wind rustling through the trees.

Ariane also seemed to notice something was amiss. She set down her bag and wrapped Ponta around her neck. Ponta gave a *kyiii* of protest, a look of confusion on its face.

I unshouldered my bag and dropped it at my feet, drawing the Holy Thunder Sword of Caladbolg and lifting the Holy Shield of Teutates.

Something was rushing through the undergrowth toward us, seemingly from all directions.

Without a word, Ariane and I stood back to back, covering each other's blind spots.

I caught a glimpse of movement before a pack of massive white wolves tore out of the bushes toward us. Each wolf was around two meters long, and they all bared their large, ferocious fangs, jaws snapping in anticipation.

I swung my blade horizontally through two of the leaping attackers, only to slice cleanly through the air as the wolf dissipated in a cloud of mist.

I yelled out in surprise. "What the hell?"

Another wolf leaped toward me. It closed in fast, making my sword useless, so I punched it in the head. I didn't have time to put much strength behind the blow, but the wolf still howled as it tumbled backwards.

"Graoooowl!"

Before I could even get my bearings, I was attacked again, this time on my other side. Two wolves were throwing their bodies against my shield.

I swung my shield down, but just like the first wolf, these two turned to mist. I felt a wolf bite down hard on my sword hand, twisting wildly as if to rip my whole arm off. There was no pain, thanks to my Belenus Holy Armor, but the fact that it could throw me around so easily was still quite troubling.

I lifted my arm, and the wolf along with it, and used centrifugal force to throw it into the air, thrusting my sword up after it. Unfortunately, I'd thrown it a little too hard, and I was only able to score a glancing blow on its front leg, resulting in a light spray of blood.

I put some distance between myself and the pack, then focused on the tip of my blade and summoned Fire, sending a wave of flames toward the real and phantom wolves as they readied themselves for another attack. The spell roasted everything in its path and raised the temperature of the surrounding air by a few degrees.

I tried to use Dimensional Step to flank the wolves, but they were moving too fast for me to find an empty space to teleport to. I couldn't have picked a worse time to discover such a limitation to my teleportation.

I glanced behind me to find Ariane easily handling her own pack—both real and phantoms. She made the most of her spirit magic, keeping her front clear with fire and easily injuring any wolves that came close enough to strike. She'd stabbed one of the wolves in the eye and severed a tendon in its leg, preventing it from moving. The other wolves were all similarly injured, their white fur mottled with blood.

I was truly impressed by her fighting prowess, built up over many years serving as a soldier. Even with all of my power, I was only able to stand my ground through brute force alone. In a battle against multiple opponents, my shortcomings were all too apparent.

I could probably take out the whole lot of them if I used an area-of-effect spell, but I hadn't tested that kind of magic in this world yet. Not only might I inadvertently end up harming Ariane, but using an attack like that so recklessly could also cause significant damage to the forest. I was already worried about the flames I was using to hold the wolves back, but fortunately, nothing had caught fire so far.

There had to be something I could do...

My mind raced for some way to get the upper hand when suddenly my eyes locked on one of the wolves, deep in the pack. This wolf wasn't joining in the battle. It was hanging near the back, its attention on me. Up until now, I'd overlooked this one, distracted by all of the wolves rushing toward me.

The leader of the pack emitted a low growl as it watched the battle unfold. The area around it was clear, giving me a perfect spot to focus on. I'd only get one chance to strike it down and end this battle.

I looked beyond the pack of wolves held back by my Fire, focusing on a spot to the right of the leader. Then I cast Dimensional Step.

As soon as I disappeared, the pack of wolves froze. At that very same instant, I was appeared next to the pack leader, bringing my sword down toward it.

Somehow, the leader sensed the motion of my blade and darted back into the pack. Refusing to let it get away, I used Dimensional Step again to give chase.

Since it bounded into the air to avoid my previous

attack, I estimated how far it'd travel and then teleported to the spot where it'd land. The wolf saw me and tried to twist out of the way midair, but it was all for naught. My sword sliced easily through its throat. It let out a gurgling howl as it slammed into the ground.

A geyser of blood rained down, staining the ground red. I quickly teleported back to my place beside Ariane.

I raised my sword against the pack of wolves, but they were no longer attacking. They'd seen my mysterious powers, and they chose to turn tail and run.

"Arc, I need at least one more!"

"Roger!"

I threw my shield to the side and summoned up my Rock Shot ability, sending rocks hurtling out of my left hand into the path of the escaping wolves. The rocks exploded like grenades as soon as they hit the ground, peppering the trees and earth with stone shards and sending dirt into the air. Through the frenzy, I spotted a wolf that had been stricken by the attack and fallen.

"Dimensional Step!"

I teleported in front of the injured wolf and cleaved off its hind legs.

The wolf let out a blood-curdling howl and rolled around on the ground. I thrust my blade into its throat, but I must have struck vertebrae. There was an awful snapping noise, and I felt my sword catch for a moment before the wolf's rapid panting ceased.

And so I was able to secure Ariane's third catch of the day.

Still, I had a lot to learn from this battle.

I knew I needed to get serious about my training. I was too direct in my fighting style—I tended to get flustered and neglect all of the skills I had at my disposal. I laughed as I remembered a certain blue robot cat and all the incredibly useful gadgets he had at his disposal.

I thought back on the brutal training session I'd had with Glenys. Maybe I'd ask Ariane to help me work on my swordsmanship.

The dark elf returned her sword to its sheath and ran over to me, examining the lifeless wolf at my feet.

"Thank you, Arc! I never would have imagined that we could take down three haunted wolves! This will be a wonderful gift for my sister."

I was captivated by her brilliant smile, much brighter than anything I'd seen on her face thus far. She tilted her head to the side, confused by my lack of response. I broke the silence with a cough, struggling to turn the conversation around.

"So...these are the haunted wolves I've heard so much about? Their tails certainly glow, I suppose, but not as much as I expected..."

I looked down at the dead wolf, but its tail only gave off a faint glimmer.

Ariane stroked it, checking the quality of the fur as she spoke. "That's because there's very little mana energy in this forest. If you take it back to Canada, it'll emit a beautiful blue light."

Ponta, still wrapped around Ariane's neck and much calmer now that the fighting was over, gave its body a shake, puffing out its fur.

"I'm really sorry to ask this of you, but could you use Transport Gate to take us back to Lalatoya really quick? I'd like to get the work on these started."

I took a look at our surroundings. "That's fine, but...if I use Transport Gate to return to Lalatoya, we'll need to start our trip to Houvan all over again from Selst. That is, unless there's some sort of unique and memorable location nearby."

Transport Gate, my long-distance teleportation spell, would only allow me to teleport to a place that I had committed to memory. Out here in the forest, surrounded by endless trees, there was simply no way for me to pinpoint a location.

"Hmm, all right. Maybe you could look for someplace nearby that you could teleport back to while I prepare the wolves' bodies?"

"Good plan. I'll start looking then."

After retrieving my shield and dusting off my cloak, I began my search.

Seeing me start to leave, Ponta dove from Ariane's shoulders and flew up to my helmet. Apparently, we were going together.

If there was some sort of notable landmass or building, I could use that to return here from Lalatoya using Transport Gate. However, if I just haphazardly wandered off into the woods looking for such a landmark, I might never find my way back to Ariane. I needed to pick a direction and head in a straight line.

I launched myself forward using Dimensional Step, searching for anything unique. But everywhere I looked, there were just trees, grass, dirt, and rocks. Nothing seemed particularly memorable.

From time to time, I came across blood-stained underbrush or tracks from the haunted wolves. They must have made their escape this way. Given their hasty retreat, it seemed unlikely that I'd run into them at my current pace, but I still proceeded with caution.

I glanced up at the small patches of sky I could make out between the branches and leaves. Ominous gray clouds blanketed the forest in darkness. I looked behind me, but Ariane had long since faded into the deep shadows of the forest.

Imagining how easy it would be for me to get lost, I broke off a few branches from a nearby tree and shoved them into the ground at regular intervals so I could find my way back.

Ponta spotted some berries from its vantage atop my head and cried out. Since we certainly weren't starving to death, and I didn't particularly want to get lost in the woods chasing after fruit, I decided to ignore its cries.

After walking a bit farther, comforting Ponta all the while, I suddenly heard a sound like someone talking. I stopped to listen.

Amid the trees swaying in the breeze and the cries of animals in the distance, I could faintly hear people bustling about.

The sound was slightly off my set trajectory. If changed direction now, I'd need to leave another marker behind. I ripped several more branches off a nearby tree and stabbed them into the ground in a circle.

That should be good enough.

I made sure Ponta was secure on my head and started walking in the direction of the voices.

As I moved through the forest, I distantly held out hope that I might be headed toward some sort of unique building.

The sounds grew louder, but it soon became apparent

that I wasn't just overhearing some sort of boisterous conversation—there was a fight in progress.

From up ahead, the wind carried the sounds of anger, sadness, and fear. I caught the scent of blood, mixed with the stench of something burning. I had a bad feeling about this.

I wrapped Ponta around my neck, took several deep breaths, and made my way toward the clash of battle ahead.

The forest opened up into a narrow path, bordered on its left by a small embankment. A wall of trees ran across the top, their roots compacting the earth. Thick bushes sprouted beyond that, making it impossible to see any farther.

A massive black carriage, drawn by a team of four horses, made its way along the forest path. The carriage was adorned with an elegant design, showcasing the true skill of the craftsman who'd made it. Its owner must have been wealthy indeed. Knights on horses and other soldiers surrounded the carriage—an enormous force of more than fifty men devoted to its protection. Each man walked with his gear held tight, well-trained and vigilant.

Amid this procession sat a man dressed in an impressive suit of armor, riding atop a majestic horse. The young man had immaculately combed brown hair and kept his square jaw parallel to the ground, his head on a constant pivot as he surveyed his surroundings. The man's name was Rendol du Frivtran—the son of Duke Frivtran, one of the seven dukes of Rhoden Kingdom. He was charged with ensuring the safety of the contents of the carriage.

Even this many soldiers would have been far too few to protect a member of the nobility. However, the more men they brought with them, the slower the pace, so they'd taken the bare minimum in the interest of speed.

The procession's mission was to get the carriage's occupant to the Grand Duchy of Limbult as fast as possible without letting anyone find out. This was why they'd decided to avoid any major towns, and were taking alternative routes instead. They would need to be on the lookout for stray monsters and bandits this way, but it was unlikely that anyone they encountered would be able to cut through fifty of their best men.

Rendol, however, didn't let his guard down for even a second. Of course, that didn't mean he could slow their pace, either. They'd already been traveling for a day and a half.

A young woman looked out from the window of the carriage, catching brief glimpses of the gray sky above through gaps in the trees. Yuriarna, second princess to the Rhoden Kingdom, let out a sigh. At just sixteen years old, she already gave the appearance of a dignified noble, in spite of her youthful complexion. She ran her fingers through her light blond hair, betraying her anxiety. Next to her, her chambermaid offered her some baked sweets.

"Miss Yuriarna, maybe eating a little something might help calm you down. Are you worried about this visit to Limbult?"

The woman sitting at Yuriarna's side was her chambermaid, Ferna, who had been with the worried young noble ever since she was a little girl. Yuriarna shook her head and turned away the treat, concern etched on her face.

"The closer we get, the tighter my heart grows. I know there's no way they could catch up with us at this pace, but still..."

Yuriarna was practically speaking to herself at this point. She turned her attention back to the window. The sky looked like it was about to start weeping, as if the turmoil she felt inside had reached the clouds themselves. She shut her eyes.

At that very moment, screams of horror and anger began echoing from the procession's front lines.

"We're under attack!"

Rendol rode up beside the carriage and began issuing orders, urging his troops to mount an offensive. The whole force surged forward as one, forming a well-trained defensive line to protect the carriage.

After checking on his men, Rendol turned his gaze to the front lines, glaring at the enemy beyond. Obviously, someone had been tipped off. There was no other way to explain an ambush. They'd left the capital in secret and maintained a high pace throughout the journey.

This frustrated Rendol greatly, but he didn't have time to worry about that right now.

It was obvious that these were no mere bandits, though he couldn't say for sure if they were affiliated with the first or second prince. Several mages let loose with Fire Beretta attacks on his front lines.

Few bandits would have such magic at their disposal.

"They have mages! All knights with mythril shields, block the magical attacks!"

On Rendol's command, a group of knights pulled up their shields and rushed to the front while the archers hung back and lobbed arrows at the enemy. As Rendol's men surged forward, a volley of arrows sailed over their heads, felling the guards protecting the rear.

The soldiers grew visibly terrified at this second

ambush, but Rendol ordered them to remain calm. Fortunately, they were in the middle of a forest, which forced the enemy to shoot in a straight line, limiting their range to the rear guard.

Nearly a hundred men in bandit gear appeared at the rear of the column, though the way they moved made it apparent that they all had military training.

"I want thirty men protecting the rear! Don't let the bandits get close. The rest of you, stay close to the carriage and clear the path up front! We must protect the carriage at all costs!"

The force split in two, moving as ordered.

Considering how massively outnumbered they were, Rendol decided to send a minimal force up front to take out the mages and focus on getting the carriage away. But for some reason, the forces he'd sent to protect the rear were moving far more slowly than usual, creating a gap in the line.

A wave of frustration and anxiety washed over Rendol.

The man leading the rear ambush smiled devilishly as he watched the soldiers split. "Fire another volley into their ranks!"

A squad of archers dressed in bandit attire nocked, drew, and loosed their arrows. The arrows flew toward the knights and soldiers protecting the carriage's rear.

Though they scored some glancing blows, they failed to cause any critical injuries. However, the guards who were struck by arrows were noticeably slower now, and were having a harder time maintaining a defensive posture.

"Break through their defense and kill the princess!"

The faux bandits responded to his command in unison, launching a full-on assault against the men attempting to hold the line. The attack on the narrow forest path was intense.

The lethargic men were struck down first, one after the next—an unbecoming end for elite soldiers who'd been handpicked to guard the princess.

"Sir Kaecks, the guards aren't moving like they should. What happened?"

A short man in priestly robes addressed the bandit-at-tired commanding officer. He hardly gave the impression of a holy man, however, as he gleefully watched the guards fall.

"This is the great reveal, Boran."

The black-haired man disguised as a bandit, whom Boran had referred to as Kaecks, wore a sinister grin on his sharp, unshaven face, giving him the appearance of a real ruffian. However, the leather armor that protected his body, and the sword that hung from his waist, made it clear that this was not the case. Kaecks Coraio du Brutios—son of the Duke Brutios, one of the seven dukes of Rhoden—commanded this raid at his father's behest. Duke Brutios was one of the first prince's supporters.

Kaecks handed Boran an arrow. Boran accepted it, though it looked no different from any other arrow he'd seen.

"The arrowheads have been dipped in a very rare poison that can only be found inside a giant basilisk. Instead of simply killing their targets immediately, these arrows paralyze them."

The priest could barely contain his excitement. "Ooh! You've come prepared, I see!"

"We happened across a basilisk recently, so we only had time to prepare a limited supply. However, a small breach in their defense is all we need."

The two men turned their attention back to the battle, where the soldiers guarding the carriage were falling *en masse*. They watched the man leading the defense urging his men to break through the mages.

Rendol stood next to the carriage, issuing orders to the defenders under his command. He cursed as his men to the rear fell one after another, his mood growing increasingly dark. He'd never imagined his knights and soldiers could be defeated so easily.

The knights absorbed the assault from the enemy mages

with their mythril shields, trying to take the offensive. All of a sudden, the mages drew back. In their place, fifty more enemies appeared to attack the over-extended soldiers.

Rendol knew it was only a matter of time until the rear guard fell. He was running out of options. "All knights, prepare your Exploding Spheres!"

On Rendol's command, the knights sheathed their swords, each pulling a single sphere from the leather pouches on their backs while continuing to hold their shields against the magical onslaught.

The attacking soldiers' eyes went wide. Those in the front scrambled over each other as they attempted to get away, while those behind held fast, unable to see what all the fuss was about. The men crammed together in the narrow road.

"Move it, you idiot! Get outta the way!!!"

Rendol made the most of this temporary advantage as the attackers descended into chaos. "And...throw!!!"

"Blow 'em to smithereens!"

At Rendol's command, the knights murmured a spell in unison, then hurled the magical spheres at the enemy.

The spheres arced through the air, landing in the middle of the enemy formation, where they exploded on impact. An enormous, roaring blast blew the nearest soldiers away. The remaining men broke ranks and ran, leaving the mages defenseless. Rendol saw his opening.

"Push the assault and get that carriage through! All men, to me!!!" Rendol snapped his reins, charging into the fray.

The knights deflected the mages' fresh barrage of Fire Beretta and Rock Shot with their mythril shields and pushed into the enemy lines. Those on horseback cut down the remaining fighters, tearing a deep hole in the formation.

A stray Fire Beretta struck Rendol's horse, sending him to the ground. His knights tumbled unceremoniously from their own horses as they tried desperately not to trample their commander. The enemy soldiers who'd survived the explosive attack rushed in to slash the throats and stomachs of the dismounted knights, killing them where they stood.

Rendol managed to pull himself up, only to discover that his leg was broken and wouldn't support his weight.

A man with a short spear and hideous grin stabbed him in the side.

"Gwaaaaargh!"

Blood spilled from Rendol's mouth as he screamed in pain, his hands flying to the wound. His eyelids fluttered, his vision growing cloudy as he desperately searched for the carriage he'd sworn to protect. The last thing he saw was a large man in bandit attire standing in front of the carriage, yanking the door open.

The man gripped a blood-drenched sword in one hand as his ripped the door open with the other. A young chambermaid dove out with dagger in hand, aiming for his heart. The man caught the blade on his left arm, where it buried itself deep. Enraged, he punched the chambermaid in the face with all his might.

"Stupid wench!"

Ferna was thrown back into the carriage, where she slumped, motionless.

The man pulled the dagger from his arm and threw it aside, thrusting his own blade into Ferna's chest.

"Guwaugh!"

Her eyes rolled up, her blood staining the upholstery. The man kicked her limp body out of the carriage.

"Noooo! Fernaaaaaa!"

Yuriarna's childhood friend had just been murdered in front of her, drenching her elaborate gown in gore. She launched herself at the man.

He smiled as he blocked the door to the carriage. Then he took his sword, still dripping with Ferna's blood, and plunged it into the princess' chest.

Confusion flashed across Yuriarna's face. She looked down, and her eyes went wide as she saw the sword sticking out of her. Her expression grew pained, tears staining her cheeks, a voiceless scream on her lips. She coughed up bright red blood, slumping against the wall of the carriage as the life drained from her body, her brown eyes no longer seeing.

The man yanked the sword from her chest, wiped it clean on her dress, and returned it to its sheath. Then he reached down and carefully unclasped the necklace she wore. He took his prize with him as he exited the carriage.

The area was littered with the bodies of the princess' guards, who were continuing to fall, one by one.

From the rear, where he'd been watching the battle unfold, Kaecks gave the order to kill the survivors. "Show 'em what bandits can do! Any valuables we find will be added to your reward!"

The soldiers, still in their disguises, cheered at this announcement. They scoured the fallen guards for weapons and other valuables.

"You're welcome to join them, Boran." Kaecks addressed the priest, all too aware of the envious gaze the short man held as he looked out over the battlefield.

"W-well, if you insist..."

A smile broke across Boran's face as he gleefully hurried off to search for his own spoils. Kaecks glared at his back, appalled at the crassness of this particular man of the cloth.

"Sir Kaecks, a memento from Princess Yuriarna."

In spite of his large size, the man who'd just taken the princess' life had approached Kaecks silently, only making his presence known when he spoke. He held the princess' necklace in his outstretched hand.

Kaecks took it, a deranged smile gracing his lips. "Well done. It truly is unfortunate what happened to Her Highness. Still, I never would have imagined they'd bring Burst Spheres with them. We took heavy casualties."

The necklace contained a large gem encased in a gold flower, and was further decorated by many smaller gems. It had been one of many gifts from the late queen to her two daughters. After carefully wrapping the prize in a silk cloth and tucking it into his pocket, Kaecks issued the order for his soldiers to retreat.

Just then, one of the men rummaging around for loot let out a blood-curdling cry.

"Gyaaaaugh!"

Kaecks whirled in the direction of the scream. White wolves dove from the trees lining the road, one after another, tearing the nearby men to shreds. But these weren't just beasts in search of a meal.

They were out to kill.

The wolves ran from one man to the next, baring their fangs and biting indiscriminately.

The wolves moved nimbly in spite of their massive size.

Their powerful jaws and sharp teeth made quick work of the distracted soldiers.

The mages were the first to try and fight back. They began chanting, but the wolves seemed to pick up on this and swarmed the mages in a massive pack, killing them before they could summon any spells.

The men armed with swords attempted to defend as well, but whenever they scored a direct hit on one of the wolves, it simply vanished in a puff of smoke, distracting them long enough for another wolf to take them down from behind.

Princess Yuriarna's hunters had now become the hunted. Kaecks watched numbly as the brutal scene unfolded before him. The large man beside him put a name to the hellish demons. "Haunted wolves…"

This snapped Kaecks back to his senses. "Full retreat! All men, form back up! Supply squad, break out the shields! Burn everything else down to the ground! Let the horses go. They'll distract the wolves!"

The soldiers didn't need to be told twice. The supply squad took their gear from the horses, giving each one a swift slap to send it running before unpacking their massive shields. Since speed had been of the utmost priority for this mission, there were only so many shields to go around. Several soldiers had to huddle behind each one.

"Fall back! Retreeaat!"

Kaecks issued the final order, ignoring the stragglers who hadn't made it back to their lines.

"Dammit, how many of them are there?"

There looked to be at least fifteen haunted wolves terrorizing his men, though clearly not all of them were real.

Kaecks glowered at the scene in front of him. "I'm guessing each haunted wolf can create two or three apparitions. There must be at least five of them out there."

The men slowly retreated, grateful to escape these gods of death with their lives. As the number of men assembled behind the shield wall grew, relief washed over the group, though it didn't approach the level of excitement they'd shown only moments ago while looting.

Fortunately, the haunted wolves only seemed interested in the soldiers surrounding the carriage. They paid no attention to the escaping men.

Once free of the forest and out of sight of the wolves, the soldiers broke into cheers. Kaecks felt the tension melt from his shoulders.

However, as he surveyed his remaining men, a wave of intense grief wracked his body. Over half of his soldiers had been lost in the ambush and subsequent wolf attack.

The clouds hung heavy and dark in the sky as I made my way through the oppressive forest toward the sounds of battle.

They died down before I reached the source, however, replaced with the increasingly acute smell of blood. Soon, my own movements through the trees were the loudest sounds around me.

I stepped through a row of bushes and found a long path running through the forest. I was standing atop a three-meter-tall embankment running parallel to a path. The immediate area was littered with bodies, the scent of warm blood heavy in the air.

I could tell by the craters and scorch marks everywhere that this had been an intense battle.

Amid the mountain of bodies, I found five massive white wolves gnawing on something that had once been human, the bones making an awful snapping sound. These looked like the haunted wolves that had gotten away from us earlier. One of them was wounded where Ariane had landed a glancing blow.

The wolves looked up from their fleshy feast, detecting my presence as I stepped from the bushes. They eyed me suspiciously and started to retreat.

"Grrrowl!"

I spread my black cloak out and threw both of my

hands into the air, shouting to the heavens as I returned their glare. The wolves literally jumped in surprise before turning tail and disappearing into the bushes on the far side of the path.

My attempt to scream them into submission had worked better than I thought it would, though it had also scared Ponta half to death. The poor creature started from its perch around my neck, where it had been curled like a fur scarf.

I gently patted Ponta's fur back down as it let out little mews of consternation. I scanned my surroundings.

A large black carriage sat in the middle of all the carnage. Knights clad in magnificent armor lay dead all around it, as if they'd given their lives defending whoever was inside—likely a high-ranking noble.

Of the carriage's four horses, two had been killed. The remaining two had been left to whinny and paw the ground in fear, unable to escape the thick harnesses that held them in place.

There were a large number of bandits lying around as well, though none of them seemed to be breathing. Other than the frightened neighing of the horses, the whole area was engulfed in an eerie silence.

I worried for a moment that Ariane and I had inadvertently caused this situation by letting the haunted wolves get away, but the more I looked at it, the more that seemed unlikely.

I hopped down from the embankment to the path three meters below and made my way toward the carriage, careful to not step on any of the bodies. The knights and armored soldiers had all been killed by swords and arrows, without a single trace of a wolf bite among them. A few bodies had been charred by some sort of magical attack, though the majority looked to have been killed with conventional weapons.

Putting all of this together, it seemed like the guards had already been killed at the bandits' hands by the time the wolves showed up. Though I did find evidence of a few bandits who'd been killed by the guards, the majority of them appeared to have been killed by the wolves—arms torn off at the shoulder, stomachs chewed open, and worse.

Among them, I found the body of a man in priest's robes—a holy man, apparently, though nothing was left of his head. What an awful way to die.

I put my hands together in a brief prayer for this man who'd given his entire life to God, only to have it ripped away by cruel fate. Then I turned my back on the mountain of corpses and made my way toward the carriage.

The door was hanging wide open. Beneath it lay the body of a young woman in servant's attire, her face buried in the mud. Inside the blood-stained carriage I found the body of another young woman, this one dressed in an extravagant gown. The second woman's long blond hair was stuck to her face with dried blood. A fresh sword wound gaped in her chest.

She must have been the one the guards were protecting.

Her blood was still warm, her flesh still a bit pink. Tears clung to her half-open eyes. She'd only died recently. I closed her eyelids, and she looked as if she were merely asleep.

Ponta let out a solemn cry. "Kyiii...."

I petted the fox's head absently while I ran through all the spells available to me.

It was no use to try recovery magic on someone who was already dead. However, my Bishop and Priest classes had revival spells. These were pretty common in video games, but here in the real world, I wondered if they would actually have any effect.

The mid-tier Bishop class had the Reanimation spell, which would bring someone back with one-tenth of their health. In reality, coming back to life with one-tenth of your health would probably only return you to the brink of death. You might just die again in agony.

The top-tier Priest class had access to the Rejuvenation spell, which would bring someone back to life with full health, though I was unsure how that would play out in the real world.

Still, I couldn't shake the feeling that it was too soon for this young woman to die, so I decided to give my magic a try. I reached out and held my hand over the slumped girl.

"Rejuvenation!"

Her body began to glow, a yellowish-gold light flickering across her as the wound in her chest started to close. It was like I was watching a video being played in reverse. When the light disappeared, all of the girl's injuries were gone.

In the game, like I said, the spell would recover all of your health...but I wasn't sure what that meant for all the blood the girl had lost. The floor of the carriage was still drenched in it, and her dress was stained a deep crimson.

I placed my hand on the young woman's neck. I could feel a pulse, though she was still quite pale and showed no signs of waking up. She was breathing, however, so I laid her down on the bench in the carriage and stepped outside.

I propped up the chambermaid's body and, after wiping away the dirt, cast the Rejuvenation spell once again.

Her body was enveloped in the same yellowish-gold light, and her wounds began to heal. She also began to breathe again, though like the girl in the carriage, she remained unconscious.

So…revival spells worked here, though their effects were far from immediate like they were in the game. All I could do now was pray that these revived women didn't come back as monsters, like in a certain Stephen King novel.

Bringing them back to life was one thing, but I couldn't just leave them here to be killed again by monsters…or worse. I didn't row them back up the River Styx for nothing.

I decided to revive the guards while I was at it. Being careful to avoid the bandits, I cast Rejuvenation on all the nearby soldiers. However, I soon discovered that there were limits to revival spells.

First off, the spell had absolutely no effect on people who were too hideously wounded. It didn't even activate on the poor souls who'd been burned to death, or the man without a head.

I put my hands together again in sympathy for the dead priest.

There were also a few cases where soldiers were revived only to die again. This was often true for those who'd suffered significant blood loss, though the reasons for others were less clear. One man with an arrow in his chest came back to life long enough to take a few short breaths before passing away again.

It seemed like there was a limit to the spell's power, but I couldn't tell what it was.

After trying to revive all of the guards, I put my hands on my hips and surveyed my handiwork. I'd been able to bring back about thirty of them. It wasn't the most impressive number, but I hoped it would be enough to see the carriage safely out of the forest.

All that magic expenditure had left me exhausted—a rare feeling for me. I must have overdone it with the revival spells.

I was hardly in danger of using up all my magic, even with a spell like Rejuvenation, but absent any numbers to keep track of like in the game, I could only rely on how my body felt.

Even if I did temporarily run out of magic, my Twilight Cloak would solve that problem—assuming it had the same abilities here that it did in the game.

The Twilight Cloak would replenish my magic over time. And if I stayed in one spot for a while, the replenishment speed would increase. So, theoretically, all of the magic I'd just expended was slowly coming back to me.

However, it didn't seem wise for a large, armored knight like myself to just stand around staring off into space in the middle of a blood-drenched battlefield.

I used Dimensional Step to teleport back to the

embankment and sat down in the bushes so I could keep an eye on the people I'd brought back to life, just in case something bad happened.

I broke off some branches from a nearby tree to use as cover for my helmet, since a silver suit of armor didn't exactly blend in with the forest. The gaps between the leaves gave me a good view of the road below. Now it was just a matter of waiting to make sure they got out of here okay.

It almost felt like her body was floating up from the murky depths of the sea. Sensation flooded back into her limbs, and all of a sudden she was struck by an awful stench and a tightness in her skin as her eyelids flew open. It was as if she was taking her first breath of fresh air after being buried in mud. After a heavy coughing fit, she surveyed her surroundings.

She was back in her carriage, the interior stained with blood.

Princess Yuriarna tried frantically to make sense of her confusing memories, though her mind was still too foggy to reach any conclusions. She shook her head and looked down at her body.

Her gown was drenched in blood, a hole torn in the chest.

A memory of being stabbed flickered through her mind, and she instinctively threw her hands up in front of her heart. However, even though the dress was ripped, the skin underneath was unharmed. She couldn't find any injury.

"Ferna..."

She called out for her longtime companion instinctively as she looked around the cabin.

Yuriarna's memories returned all at once. She remembered Ferna being stabbed and kicked out of the carriage. Frantically, Yuriarna scrabbled for the door.

Ferna lay on her back on the ground, a peaceful expression on her face. Her clothing was also cut open at the chest. Yuriarna stumbled out of the carriage, her heart racing as she inspected the wound. But the skin beneath the torn fabric of her chambermaid's dress was flawless—not a scratch in sight.

Relief washed over Yuriarna as she watched Ferna's plump bosom rise and fall silently. Tears ran down her cheeks, dripping onto the ground.

She still had no idea what had happened, or even what was happening right now, but she was relieved to know that Ferna was safe.

Yuriarna looked up. Amid the craters and scorched earth lay the charred remains of men who'd fought so hard to protect her, intermingled with the corpses of her attackers. It looked like a scene straight out of hell. She couldn't bear the sight of all that carnage, so she turned her attention back to Ferna.

The chambermaid's eyelids fluttered open.

"Ferna, you're alive!"

Ferna turned toward the princess' sob-choked voice. "Miss Yuriarna, wh-what happened?"

The fog in her head was slowly starting to clear. She sat up and looked around.

The surrounding area was nothing but devastation. As memories of the brutal ambush came back, Ferna turned her attention to Yuriarna and inspected the princess closely.

"Are you all right, Princess? Were you hurt?"

Yuriarna covered her mouth to hide her gentle laugh at the sudden change in her chambermaid's demeanor. "I'm fine. What about you, Ferna?"

Ferna frantically checked herself for wounds as the memory of being stabbed returned. She looked at the princess with confusion. "How am I still alive?"

Yuriarna had no answer to that. She, too, distinctly recalled having died. Her manicured eyebrows furrowed. "I don't know. I just woke up myself."

A familiar voice interrupted their conversation. "Princess! Miss Ferna! You're safe!"

The voice belonged to Rendol, the man charged with protecting the princess on her trip to the Grand Duchy. He jogged over to the carriage on unsteady legs. As soon as he reached Yuriarna, he dropped to his knees and bowed his head low.

"I'm so glad you're safe! Allow me to express my deepest regrets for failing in my duty to—"

Yuriarna cut his apology off with a flick of her hand. She stood up slowly, her light blond hair spilling down her back, and turned to face him. "Now is not the time for that, Sir Rendol."

Rendol lifted his head to look up at the princess.

"We were attacked by a force far larger than anything we anticipated. There was nothing you could have done. It is truly an act of the heavenly father that we are still alive. We can worry about what happened later. Right now, we must take action."

The look of determination on the princess' face was inspiring. Rendol wiped the tears from his eyes.

"As you wish!" He bowed his head again to the princess again.

"We're a little less than halfway to Limbult's border. There's still a very real possibility that more bandits are out there, so we will need to adjust our pace. We will proceed as originally planned, bypassing Houvan and Tiocera. Ferna, please help where you can."

"Of course, Your Highness."

With their plans reaffirmed, the three stood up and surveyed their surroundings.

Other soldiers had begun standing up from the among the bodies littering the battlefield. Seeing this sudden movement of bodies, Rendol reached for his sword. Yuriarna and Ferna ducked behind him. It wasn't uncommon in places with a large concentration of mana for corpses to come back as undead monsters and attack the living.

However, Rendol had never heard of bodies less than a day old turning undead, and definitely not in well-trafficked, low-mana places like this. It usually only happened in uninhabited magical regions.

"Rendol, wait!" Yuriarna called.

Rendol suddenly realized that the men standing in front of him were his own troops. He could hardly believe his own eyes. Several soldiers, some of whom he'd personally seen cut down on the field of battle, were now standing groggily, as if they'd just woken from a nap.

Yuriarna and Ferna stared, too, disbelief plain on their faces.

"Commander Rendol...you're all right?!" One of Rendol's soldiers—a man who'd died right in front of him—ran forward. "How'd ya make it out alive, ya scoundrel?"

The man was far from undead, and he seemed to have all of his mental faculties. Rendol looked him over several times, just to be sure his eyes weren't lying. The soldier's armor was smeared with blood, but otherwise he seemed to be unharmed, if a little pale.

Sadly, not all of his men had been spared. The charred remains of several soldiers lay still on the ground while others, unburned, remained motionless, as if in a deep slumber, even as their comrades tried to wake them.

The man in front of him kept patting his own body, as if making sure he was truly alive. "I could've sworn I was dead. What happened here?"

More soldiers started to stand, their voices blending together in a cacophony of laughter and tears as they realized they were still alive.

This was nothing short of a miracle.

"Sir Rendol..."

Yuriarna's voice brought Rendol back to the matter at hand. He turned to face the princess. No words were exchanged—the look in her eyes spoke volumes. Rendol turned back to his men.

"Atteeennntion! Princess Yuriarna will be giving a speech!"

He stepped beside her and took a knee, bowing his head in respect. The men followed Rendol's example and assumed the same pose.

"Though we may have suffered a harsh defeat at the hands of our enemies, it seems we have been spared by our heavenly father. Some of our brothers in arms, however, have been called up to serve the higher power."

Of the original fifty men charged with protecting the princess, only thirty remained to hear her words. Nearly twenty had been killed in combat. Several men wept openly at her words, their shoulders shaking.

"However, the heavens have made it clear that they wish us to proceed on our journey! We must not dwell on what has happened. Instead, let us focus our energies on the road that lies ahead and make the most of the blessing we have all been granted. We are unstoppable! Onward to Limbult!"

The soldiers let out a loud cheer.

"Hoorah!"

Rendol stood and began firing orders to his men.

"Swap out the horses and track down the ones that have escaped! At the very least, secure enough for the carriage. Arm yourselves with any weapons you can!"

The men leaped to carry out their leader's commands.

The force of around thirty men—apparently a procession for the princess—quickly assembled their gear and took the carriage off to the east. I continued to watch over them until they were small specks in the distance.

When they were completely out of sight, I spread the branches I'd been using for cover and stuck my head out. From atop my helmet, Ponta snored faintly. The cottontail fox had apparently decided to take a nap. I moved slowly, careful not to disturb its slumber.

For a while, I'd been worried about what might happen to all the people I'd revived, so I was quite relieved to see them off.

I'd figured that the young woman was some sort of nobility, but I'd had no idea she was from the royal family...or that she would interpret my simple spell as a miraculous act of god. After thinking about it for a moment, however, the ability to bring back the dead reminded me of a certain red stone a pair of alchemist brothers had searched for in an anime I used to watch.

As far as I could tell, there had been no negative side effects—like men turning undead, or going crazy.

I still wasn't sure what had prevented me from bringing all of the men back. The whole experience had left me with the impression that I should avoid using the spell too often. In the game, people were merely thankful to be revived. But here, I ran the very real risk of being seen as some sort of cleric...or worse, a god. What if someone got it into their head to form a religion around me? What if I started a holy war?

Bringing back the occasional daughter of a farmer or son of a minor noble killed in some sort of accident was all well and good, but a princess who'd been murdered... that was another thing entirely.

Without a doubt, this would be a day for the history books.

On the other hand, royal families often had many princesses. Maybe the history books would just gloss over the incident. That was my hope, anyway.

Then again, no one had actually witnessed what I'd done. In the future, I would just need to make sure I only used revival magic when absolutely necessary.

The committee in the back of my mind reached a conclusion. Protecting myself had won out over the other, dissenting voices. The overwhelming majority had voted in favor of moving forward as if nothing had changed.

"We'll just pretend that never happened."

I turned around carefully, so as not to disturb Ponta, and headed back the way I'd come. How long had it been since I left Ariane?

Following the markers I'd placed, I used Dimensional Step to move through the woods at a rapid pace. Soon, I caught sight of three wolves with their hind legs bound together hanging from a tree branch.

Sitting against the base of the tree was an amethyst-colored dark elf with a very angry look on her face.

She sat with her knees held tightly against her chest. A smile appeared on her face for the briefest moment when she saw me, though the scowl quickly returned.

"Well, you certainly took your time! How far did you go, anyway?"

I muttered the first excuse that came to mind as I stepped through the bushes and approached her. "I'm sorry. I got lost."

"Well, the blood's completely drained from the wolves. Let's head back to Lalatoya."

"Ah, that's right...I was searching for a landmark, wasn't I?" I slammed my fist into my open palm as I suddenly remembered the reason I'd left.

"Wait, you mean you were just wandering around the forest this whole time?" Ariane looked like she couldn't believe her own ears.

I could hardly argue with her criticism. She was right to be angry.

"I'm sorry. I became fixated on getting back and completely forgot about my objective. Let's head in that direction and see if we can find something." I pointed off toward the Anetto Mountains, barely visible through a gap in the trees.

I handed the sleeping Ponta over to Ariane and, before she could protest, used Dimensional Step to teleport off into the forest once more. I hoped that fox's sleeping face would have a calming effect on Ariane while I searched for a teleportation landmark.

About ten minutes later, I found myself in a small clearing. A large boulder jutted out of the grass in its center. Off to its side, a massive tree sprouted up, its branches practically hugging the boulder. This seemed like a good enough landmark.

The tree stood tall, as if it ruled the entire clearing, keeping away any other trees or branches that would dare invade its space.

If such a tree were found in Japan, it would without a doubt be surrounded by decorative ropes and talismans and treated as a holy spot.

"Well, I think this'll do the trick."

I committed the spot to memory. It was certainly an

impressive sight, so it wasn't too difficult to memorize every detail. I started back.

The sky above, or what little I could see through the dense tree cover, was covered in dark clouds. Heavy raindrops began to fall. I looked up at the weeping heavens and wondered if we might need to put off our trip after returning to Lalatoya. It would all depend on the weather.

I hurried back to Ariane and Ponta using Dimensional Step.

When I emerged from the bushes, Ariane's face was buried in Ponta's soft, fuzzy stomach, rubbing her face back and forth.

"Aww, Ponta! Your belly's soooo soft!"

"Kyuu kyuu!"

Ariane spoke with an uncharacteristically cutesy voice as she rubbed her face back and forth. Ponta cried in delight as it twisted about, probably ticklish from her nuzzling.

I watched in silence until Ariane finally noticed me.

"Oh, uh, Arc! Well, you were pretty fast this time. Did you, uh, find a landmark?"

Her amethyst cheeks took on a pink hue that I could see even from this distance. She stammered as she spoke, clearly embarrassed. I was excited to have caught a glimpse of her softer side, but I strove to keep my cool.

"Yes, there's a great location not too far from here. Depending on the weather, we may want to call it a day after we take the haunted wolves back to Lalatoya."

Ariane cleared her throat and nodded coolly at my suggestion, returning to form. Her cheeks, however, were still flushed a delicate shade of pink. "You're probably right. Since you can teleport us, there's no need to rush back into the woods if the weather's bad."

Ariane used her spirit magic to fill the shallow pit she'd dug to collect the blood from the wolves dangling above it. I helped her remove the wolves from the branch and line them up on the ground.

The creatures were a little lighter now that their blood had been drained. I was impressed that Ariane had been able to lift them onto the branch by herself...and before draining them, at that.

Ponta slapped at the haunted wolves' noses with its front paws, getting in a few good blows. Apparently, the fox got a burst of courage when its opponents were no longer moving.

"Well, off to Lalatoya. I'll give you a good belly-nuzzle later, Ponta."

"Kyiii!"

Ariane elbowed me hard in the side. When I turned, her arms were crossed and she was looking in the other direction. Even from behind, though, I could tell she was puffing out her cheeks.

Well, at least Ponta had been happy about my offer. The fox resumed its place back atop my helmet as I summoned my spell.

"Transport Gate!"

I was more careful this time, since we also had three large haunted wolves to bring with us. The pillar of light that appeared at my feet had grown from its usual three meters in diameter to four, to accommodate the added cargo. The world turned black, and the next instant, we were out of the forest and standing in front of the large tree house we'd left the previous morning. We'd made it back to Lalatoya safe and sound.

I looked down and, sure enough, the haunted wolves had teleported with us.

Apparently, if I focused a little harder when summoning Transport Gate, I could create a larger pillar and bring things along with me. That could prove rather useful. Of course, I'd need to practice more in order to perfect the technique.

"The rain's falling pretty hard here."

Ariane was right—what had started as a light drizzle in the forest was already a full-blown downpour in Lalatoya. If I didn't get out of the rain soon, my armor might fill up and start sounding like a water xylophone.

"Arc, can you wait at my house for a bit? I'm going to get some help to carry and skin the wolves."

She didn't bother waiting for a reply before running off into the village.

I took another look at the beasts lying at my feet.

The wolves' tails were no longer the pale white I'd seen in the forest. They were now glowing a distinct white-blue. It looked rather mystical out here under the cloud-covered sky. A veil made from these would truly be a sight to behold.

Ponta must have been soaked through, because I could feel it trying to shake the accumulated water from its fur.

"I'm so sorry. Let's get you out of the rain."

I knocked on the door to the tree house. A voice asked who it was and, after I replied, a confused-looking Glenys appeared.

"Oh, Arc. You're certainly back early."

"Well, Miss Ariane has acquired a present for her sister's wedding, so we came to drop it off."

Glenys's gaze fell on the beasts lying in the garden. "Haunted wolves? That's quite impressive. And three of them, at that!" She looked up at the coursing rain. "Please, come inside. I assume Ariane went off to make a deal with the hunters?"

"I believe so. Thank you for your kindness."

I stepped across the threshold and followed Glenys up to the second floor, where she poured me a cup of hot tea. I removed my drenched helmet and sipped at my drink. The liquid was light brown and tasted just like straight black tea.

Ponta sat on the chair next to me and licked its soaked fur, trying to straighten out its coat. Around my third cup of tea, the fox drifted off to sleep.

"Well, Ariane's certainly taking her time. Why don't you stay here for the night? It's raining pretty heavily now."

I looked out the dining room window. Just as she'd said, the rain was falling in sheets, hammering against the glass panes. Even though it was only around four o'clock, it was already pitch-black outside.

It would probably be some time before Ariane returned, so I figured this was a good opportunity to fulfill the dream I'd been harboring for a while now.

"Miss Glenys, I hear that you have a bath here. Would it be possible for me to use it? I'd be more than happy to pay for any costs associated with heating the water."

"The bath? Of course I don't mind! But please don't worry about paying me. Do you...need a bath?" Glenys easily acquiesced to my impassioned plea, though she looked slightly perplexed. "Well, I guess it doesn't really matter. Why don't you wash little Ponta while you're at it?"

"Of course. Ponta could use a good scrubbing."

I picked the slumbering cottontail fox up and followed Glenys down to a secluded bathhouse off the first floor. The place sat in the shadow of the large tree, obscuring it from the building's entrance.

Water was collected from a small creek and heated using a stove embedded in the massive wooden bath. However, the stove itself appeared to be magical, relying on stones for fuel, which gave it a rather modern appearance. Glenys told me that these same magical water heaters were also common among human nobles.

After she left, Ponta and I took a nice long bath. Once my weary bones had warmed up, I made my way back into the house. Just as we were sitting down to a glass of cold tea and dinner with Glenys, Ariane appeared in the dining room.

She looked taken aback to find me dressed in a traditional elven robe with Ponta sitting atop my bare skull.

"You've certainly made yourself at home."

"A bath works wonders on both mind and body!"

Lacking any skin or muscle tissue on my skull, I wasn't sure the face I was making looked like a proper smile, but Ariane seemed to pick up on it.

"That's good to hear."

Then she puffed out her cheeks, as if she'd suddenly remembered something.

"I'm locking the door to the bath from now on, just so you know!"

Arc and Ponta's Bathtime Adventure

I GOT PERMISSION FROM Ariane's mother to use the bath. It was the first chance I'd had to wash myself since coming to this world.

I followed Glenys through the house, cradling a snoring Ponta in my arms. When she opened a door down on the first floor, I was greeted by a walkway that ran through the backyard to a small building. The walkway had a roof to keep the rain off, but it lacked walls, giving me a perfect view of the backyard.

A changing room was waiting for me behind another wooden door. Off to my right stood a series of shelves packed with baskets made of interweaved vines, containing various supplies. It looked a lot like a changing room in a traditional public bathhouse back in Japan.

Glenys pulled out one of the baskets, which contained some neatly folded clothes.

"You can put these on when you're done with the bath. It must be tiring to always wear that armor, no?"

She held out an elven robe—the same that she herself was wearing—marked with a unique crest on the back.

"Much appreciated."

Glenys showed me how to tie it closed using a leather belt connected to the back. After giving me a quick rundown on how the bath worked, she left me and Ponta alone in the changing room so she could start preparing dinner.

Ponta let out a yawn and glanced around the room, waking up at last.

"Let's clean you up, buddy."

"Kyi?"

The fox tilted its head to the side in confusion. I chuckled.

I removed my gleaming Belenus Holy Armor and placed it piece by piece onto the changing room floor. There was no way it would fit into any of the baskets.

Ponta ran around and through the pieces of my armor as if they were some sort of obstacle course.

Once I'd taken everything off, I was completely bare. Even though there was nothing for me to hide on my skeletal body, I still used a small towel to cover the area where my private parts would have been.

"Huh. So...it's just like a normal bathhouse in here?"

I picked Ponta up by the scruff of the neck and set it on my shoulder.

The changing room was connected to the bath by large frosted-glass doors. The sight that greeted me on the other side was quite impressive.

"Whoa!"

The floor of the bathing area was made of textured stones. Off to my right was a bath surrounded by square posts made of exquisite wood. A light steam rose off the surface of the water. To my left, a large mirror hung from the wall, probably for washing up before entering the bath. On the ground were several stools and some wooden pails. A metal pipe jutted from the ceiling with something that looked awfully like a showerhead affixed to the end. The whole bath area was doused in warm light from a series of crystal lamps embedded in the ceiling.

For a moment, I felt like I was in the bath of a traditional Japanese inn, completely forgetting that I was in another world.

I made my way to the washing area—it was customary to clean yourself before entering the bath—and removed my towel. I twisted the bulb halfway up the U-shaped pipe and was greeted with a shower of warm water.

"Kyi! Kyiiii!"

Surprised at the sudden spray, Ponta dove off my shoulder and ran to the corner of the room. It shook its whole body, trying to get the water out of its fur.

I realized it might be a bit of a hard sell to get a wild creature like Ponta to enjoy a shower. I decided to worry about the fox later and focus on my own body first.

Warm water flowed over my skull, dripping down my lower jaw and through my empty ribcage. It continued down my spine to my pelvis, where it drained out onto the floor.

It was a very peculiar sensation, almost like urinating. But I let the water wash over my entire body, enjoying the warmth seeping into my bones.

"This feels so good!" I threw my arms out and yelled without thinking.

The green cottontail fox tensed in the corner of the room, but I didn't pay it much mind.

My gaze wandered to the top of the shelves in front of me. A hard, round, green object sat in a wooden box. I brought it up to my nose and give it a whiff. The scent of herbs assaulted me—apparently this was some kind of soap.

I tried to work up a lather, but it was practically

impossible without any flesh on my hands. The soap simply scraped against my bones.

I glanced over to Ponta, who was starting to show some interest in the bath, dipping its front feet into the water and splashing around. Watching Ponta's beautiful green fur coat sway from side to side gave me an idea. The fox was too fixated on the bath to notice as I walked up behind it, snatching it up with my left hand. I used my right hand to draw some water into the wooden pail I'd brought with me and promptly dumped it over Ponta.

"Kyiiiiiiii?!"

Ponta's delicate, poofy green fur was now sopping wet and clung close to its body, making the fox look half its normal size. I splashed water over my tense companion a few more times, until it looked like a deflated balloon.

I took Ponta back with me to the washing area and began rubbing the soap into its fur.

"Let's wash you up, huh?"

I gave Ponta a thorough scrub, working up a nice, thick lather of soap. My partner had transformed from a deflated furball into a loofah. The fox looked up at me with uncertain eyes, so I leaned in and blew on it, sending bubbles flying off into the air. One of them floated all the way up to the ceiling and caught the light of the crystal lamps, casting a rainbow down upon us.

"Kweee!"

Excited by the show, Ponta batted its paws around, trying to catch the bubbles as they drifted through the air. The more it moved, the more bubbles went flying off. Ponta—a giant bubble in its own right—took off after the rainbow-colored spheres that floated about the room.

I looked down at the bubbles in my hand and smiled. It had all gone according to plan.

As I worked the lather from Ponta into my skeletal frame, I reminded myself to ask Glenys if they had a brush or something for future baths. I couldn't keep using Ponta like this.

I let my gaze drift downward, where I caught sight of a brush with a sponge made out of a gourd attached to the end. Somehow, I had totally overlooked this. Ponta seemed to be having fun playing with the bubbles, however, so I didn't feel too bad. I'd just use the brush from now on.

I washed the soap from my body, shaping the last of the lather into an elaborate hairdo on top of my head. The skeleton that faced me in the mirror wore a soapy afro atop its head. If my soap hair were black, I'd look almost exactly like a musician from a certain popular pirate manga back in my world. I snickered to myself and turned around to show off my new appearance.

"Hey, Ponta, what do you thi—whoa!"

Ponta gave me a quick glance before summoning up a magical gust of wind and flying toward me. The spirit creature collided with my soap hair, its wind continuing on throughout the bathhouse, creating a tornado of bubbles.

"Kweeee! Kyiii!"

"It's a bubble hurricane!"

Ponta squealed as it tumbled about in its magic tornado. I got caught up in the excitement and threw out my own arms, twisting my skeletal body into various superhero poses in front of the mirror.

The room was now completely covered in bubbles.

A shiver ran up my spine as I thought of what Glenys would say to me if she found the bath like this. I could still see the smile on her face as she held the wooden practice sword out toward me. Yep, I definitely needed to make sure the place was spotless, or she might never let me use the bath again.

I filled a pail with water and splashed it across the floor and walls. I grabbed Ponta by the scruff of the neck as it tried to run past me and washed the soap from both of our bodies. Ponta growled low in its throat as the warm water splashed over it, apparently enjoying the sensation.

"Kyiiiiii..."

After cleaning up the room, I picked Ponta up and headed for the bath.

"Aaaaah..."

Barely any water splashed out as I slid into the water, thanks to how little space my bones actually took up. The warmth instantly seeped into me, causing me to let out an audible sigh. This, combined with the pleasant scent of the wood, completely relaxed me.

The bath itself was exquisitely put together—I couldn't find a single seam, despite the fact that it was a perfect square. It had probably been made by the same artisans who'd built the wall surrounding the village.

I rested the back of my skull on the edge and let my body loosen up. Ponta wasn't able to stand in the deep water, so I set it atop my ribs. After a few moments, the fox started doggy-paddling around the water, summoning up the occasional gust of wind to slide across the surface like a hovercraft.

I let out a loud yawn as I watched Ponta play. I probably looked like the skeleton of some long-forgotten person who'd died in the bath.

"I might just fall asleep right here."

After finishing its game, Ponta glided back across the water to my chest and scrambled back atop my skull.

It gave its entire body a massive shake, sending droplets of water in every direction.

"Hyak?! Blech! Cut that out, will ya?"

I plucked up the damp furball and rose from the water.

"I should probably get out before I overheat."

Considering I didn't actually have any blood running through my bones, this seemed a remote possibility. However, I didn't want to leave Ponta in the water for too long.

I stepped out of the bath and used the towel I'd brought with me to dry my body. It was a lot harder to wipe water from the gritty bones than my usual smooth skin.

Once that was done, I dried Ponta off and made my way back to get dressed.

A sudden chill washed over me as I stepped out of the warm, moist bath and into the dry air of the changing room.

I took a quick look around. Unfortunately, there was no milk waiting for me. That would have made the whole experience perfect. But I figured I could just ask Glenys for something to drink once I got back to the main house.

I sat on the bench in the changing room and let out a sigh. Overall, today had been a great day.

After rearranging its fur in the corner of the room, Ponta summoned up a light gust of wind to dry itself the rest of the way.

I was just thinking that I didn't need a hair dryer when I suddenly heard steps on the walkway. A moment later, the door opened, and someone stepped inside.

We locked eyes.

The well-proportioned, amethyst-skinned woman in front of me had let her long, white hair loose. She held a large towel in her hand. Her golden eyes went wide, her eyebrows raised in surprise.

"A skeleton..."

She dropped the towel and immediately reached for a sword that wasn't there, out of habit.

I jumped up to my feet, surprised by Ariane's sudden reaction. I had no idea she'd even returned.

"Wait, Miss Ariane! It's me, Arc!"

I'd never taken my armor off in front of her before, so she must not have put together that the skeleton in her bathhouse was me. Even though I was able to clear up this misunderstanding, Ariane quickly kicked me out, her cheeks flushed with embarrassment over her mistake.

The ending might have been less than ideal, but overall, I was satisfied with my time in the bath.

I made my way back to the dining room in search of Glenys, to see if I could get something to drink.

CHAPTER 3

The Houvan Uprising

Houvan, in the Rhoden Kingdom.

Count Fulish du Houvan's domain was located among the mountains that ran from north to south across the Rhoden Kingdom. It had been established along the route that connected the capital of Rhoden with the Grand Duchy of Limbult—the only human civilization that still maintained a trade relationship with the elves.

The many magical items produced by the elves were superior in both their performance and usefulness to anything the humans made, making them incredibly popular among human nobility. Houvan to the north and Tiocera to the south served as convenient lodgings for the many caravans that traveled along the trade route, bringing items to the kingdom's northern border.

The count's castle sat in the middle of the town of Houvan. Deep inside, its owner was speaking passionately in one of his palatial rooms. Magical crystal lamps illuminated the magnificent decorations and art that adorned it.

A middle-aged man paced back and forth across the room, alternating between agitation and abject fear as he surveyed his surroundings. He was clearly uneasy about something. His lustrous blond hair, as fine as silk, was neatly tied back at the base of his scalp. His silk shirt was adorned with intricate designs and accompanied by an equally exquisite pair of pants embroidered with gold thread. This man was none other than Count Fulish du Houvan, the ruler of this domain.

However, in spite of the opulence of the room he found himself in, the count looked incredibly dissatisfied with his surroundings, like a fish out of water. His elderly retainer raised his voice.

"Count Fulish, the merchants are filing complaint after complaint. Forcing them to undergo such stringent inspections forces them to waste time entering town. If we keep this up, shipments will slow to a crawl."

A vein bulged on Fulish's forehead. "Shut up! I must prevent the elves from getting into Houvan at all costs! Or...maybe you're colluding with them to get rid of me?"

A look of fear washed over the count's face.

Just the other day, he'd learned that the elves might be responsible for Marquis du Diento's assassination. He wasn't about to lower his guard.

Part of the problem was that he'd also purchased an elf through a slave trader. Assuming the stories about Diento's untimely demise were true, then it seemed clear that his murder had been part of a larger plot. The elves had rescued their friends and taken revenge on the man responsible for keeping the slave trade a secret.

Fortunately, the town of Houvan was located on a strategic route that ran north to south across the Rhoden Kingdom. The towering walls and well-stocked fortress would repel any intruders, so long as thorough inspections on those entering continued.

This all assumed, of course, that there weren't already sympathizers on the inside. The count's glare intensified.

"Don't be absurd! I'm simply saying that if the transport of goods to the capital is delayed any further, then it may look like we bear some sort of malice toward the royal family."

A look of understanding finally crossed Fulish's face, though it was quickly replaced by one of fear. "N-no! I absolutely will not lessen the security. If the inspections are taking too long, then we'll add more guards to perform them!"

"But that will further burden the treasury!"

No sooner had the words left the man's mouth than Fulish raised his voice in anger. "In that case, either raise taxes or levy new ones! That will take care of your little money problem!"

"W-wait! If we raise taxes any more, the people won't like it."

Fulish ran his fingers through his blond hair, then ripped the toupee from his head and threw it to the ground. "Why do I need to care what the people think? Since when did they become my equals?! If they don't want to fall in line, then we'll teach them some manners. That's your job, is it not? Now get out of my sight!"

The bald man stood there, flushed with anger, his voice now ragged. He waved his hand in annoyance toward the old man, dismissing him.

The retainer bowed his head and made for the door. As he closed it behind him, he heard the sound of a chair being thrown across the room.

"Dammit! What are we going to do about that elf?!"

Fulish chewed at his thumbnail as he mumbled to himself, lost in thought.

The elf woman he spoke of was currently locked in the dungeon.

He thought about disposing of her, but if a group of

rescuers *did* come looking for their comrade, he'd have nothing to bargain with.

On the other hand, it was against royal decree to engage in the buying and selling of elves. He couldn't just give her away, or even let her go, without fear of retribution.

For now, he decided to treat the elven woman a little better. Maybe improve her impression of him by moving her from the dungeon to one of the well-furnished rooms upstairs.

Just to be on the safe side, though, he decided to keep the mana-eater collar on her, along with the chained weights on her ankles.

He spared no expense when it came to his own protection. Unfortunately, that meant he didn't notice the fire and smoke rising from the castle around him until it was far too late.

Early the next morning, I used Transport Gate to teleport us back to the large rock—our save point—that I'd found the previous day.

We made easy progress through the forest and arrived at Houvan around noon. It actually wasn't far from where I'd discovered the princess.

The town of Houvan was located at the mouth of a valley at the base of the Anetto Mountains. To its south, the Telnassos mountain range provided a beautiful backdrop. Due to expansive forests in the foothills of both mountain ranges, cultivated lands surrounding the town spread far off to the east and west.

Houvan looked different from any other town I'd seen thus far. Rather than having a typical circular wall surrounding it, the walls were squared off, giving it the appearance of a fortress.

Yesterday's rain was long forgotten and the sun was high in the sky, almost blinding me as it reflected off the stone walls.

I put Ponta atop my head and walked with Ariane through the fields on the raised dirt path toward Houvan. The closer we got, the more apparent the sheer scale of the town became.

The fifteen-meter-high walls were surrounded by a water-filled moat. Towers stood on either side of the main gate, manned by guards who carefully watched the movements of anyone coming or going.

A stone bridge extended across the moat to the gate, where people and wagons waiting to enter the town had to undergo thorough inspections. A large line had already formed.

The town's northern gate was only barely wide enough to fit two horse-drawn carts side-by-side. I figured that was because the gates along the east to west trade route were more widely used, and probably much larger.

However, it soon became apparent that the east and west gates were even more crowded. From time to time, we'd see a cart making its way up to the north gate from either side of the city.

At the gate itself, the guards upturned entire carts, throwing open the cloaks of any passengers to inspect their faces. No exceptions were made for mercenaries, who were all required to remove their helmets before entering.

It looked to me like they were searching for some*one* rather than some*thing*.

I turned to Ariane. There was no way we'd be able to sneak in like this.

The Rhoden Kingdom had entered into a treaty that forbade the hunting of elves. However, whether anyone enforced that treaty was another story entirely. If anyone learned that my companion was a dark elf—one of the more highly prized elves—our mission would be over before we could blink.

We'd found the name of a man who lived here, a certain Fulish du Houvan, written on the elf purchase contracts.

Judging by his name, I assumed that he was a noble. If this law-violating, elf-trading noble somehow noticed that Ariane was in town, things would probably turn ugly.

As for me, I was nothing but a skeleton under my armor. There was no way I could take my helmet off during an inspection, even if the guards demanded it.

"Looks like we won't be entering through the front door."

"You're probably right."

Ariane's golden eyes peered out at the town from within her dark gray cloak.

But this didn't mean that our mission was over. We just needed to find a way to sneak into Houvan.

Ariane, Ponta, and I made our way along the town wall from the busy north entrance off toward the east, looking for a spot with no guards or other people. We eventually came to a gate many times larger than the north gate, though still relatively small. Due to its size, the foot and wagon traffic backed up past the bridge and down the road. We decided to avoid the heavy crowding at the east gate and continue south along the wall.

The south gate was relatively small, and was apparently only used for farmers going to and from the fields. There were almost no people, save for a few field workers.

The peasants of Houvan, much like those in other towns, looked exhausted. However, their tired expressions quickly turned fearful when they caught sight of us. They seemed to be more afraid of me than Ariane. I wondered if my helmet was the problem. Even though I'd been able to hide my impressive armor under my black cloak, the gleaming silver of my helmet still peeked out. There was just no way to cover it.

But as long as the peasants were willing to simply avert their eyes and not cause us any trouble, that was good enough for me.

"Miss Ariane, we will teleport into the town from here. Hold on to me."

I scanned our surroundings to make sure no one was watching.

"All right." Ariane grabbed ahold of my shoulder.

"Dimensional Step!"

Our surroundings changed in a flash as I summoned the transportation spell. An instant later, we found ourselves huddled atop the wall that ran around the town.

Obviously, we'd be spotted if stayed there, so I cast about for a place within the town limits we could teleport down to. All of the houses near the south gate seemed rather decrepit, nothing like the rich dwellings located elsewhere. I spied a particularly dilapidated house and summoned Dimensional Step again. We appeared in an alley behind the house.

"And we're finally in Houvan."

Ariane did a quick check of our surroundings before turning back to the task at hand.

"Now we just need to find the buyer, a man named Fulish du Houvan."

"Judging by his name, I'm guessing he's the ruler of this town. The castle is probably the best place to start our search."

It wouldn't do us much good to go around town asking for information about the illegal kidnapping of elves. The best and fastest way to get information would probably be to go to his residence directly.

Of course, first we needed to find out where this man lived. Heading toward the castle at the center of the town named after him seemed like a safe bet.

We moved out from behind the dilapidated building and looked around. The street was lined with similarly neglected wooden houses.

Several people nearby noticed us. Their faces tensed and they quickly moved away, disappearing between the buildings.

It again seemed to me like they were responding to seeing a helmeted knight in their midst, but I couldn't say for sure. Maybe knights in Houvan were exceptionally brutal?

After walking a short ways, we came upon a busy street lined with shops, the air filled with the cries of merchants hawking wares. The town had suddenly come to life, with people and carts jostling about.

A tense atmosphere seemed to hang over everyone, from the occasional cluster of rabble-rousers to large groups of guards. Between the inspections at the gate and the mood of the town, I couldn't help but wonder what had happened here.

Ariane and I spoke in whispers as we looked around.

"It feels pretty strange here..."

"With all the guards hanging around town, it's going to be hard to get anywhere."

As we reached the center of town, the castle walls came into view.

This certainly looked like the estate of whoever was in charge. The walls were as high as those surrounding the town, blocking off any view of the other side. A large moat ran around the wall, preventing anyone from getting too close.

The drawbridge was currently down, and a large number of guards crowded near the gate. The townspeople were all giving the area a wide berth. If we were to wander over, it seemed all too likely that we'd find ourselves being questioned at swordpoint.

We walked along the moat, trying to find a way in.

Unfortunately, guards were posted at regular intervals, and there were even more patrolling the wall itself. There were just too many people around to make teleporting in even remotely feasible.

The only other option would be to wait for nightfall and cross the wall under cover of darkness. However, if there wasn't enough moonlight to see by, it would be hard to focus on a specific point to teleport to.

All I could do was hope it didn't rain like it had the day before. Right now it was sunny out, with only a few clouds in the sky, so maybe my concerns would come to nothing.

The sound of an argument broke out from somewhere off in the distance. I turned in the direction of the voices and spotted several guards punching a young boy. A large group of people stood by, watching the events unfold from a distance, though no one seemed particularly alarmed.

"Watch where yer walkin', kid!"

"We don't need yer kind around here, ya little eyesore!"

"Admit it, you were here to steal some food, weren't ya?! Out with it!"

The guards spit epithets at the boy, who was now curled up on the ground as they barraged him with kicks.

The boy—maybe thirteen or fourteen years old—had long, scraggly black hair and was dressed in dirty, tattered clothes. Blood poured from his mouth, probably from a well-placed kick, and he looked to be in a lot of pain, though he fixed his assailants with a defiant glare. This, however, only seemed to anger the guards further.

"Whaddya lookin' at, ya little peasant brat?!"

The whole scene was hard to watch.

Right as one of the guards was about to lay into the boy with another round of kicks, I spoke up.

"Don't you think that's enough? He's just a kid."

"Who the hell are you?! Mind your own business, you..."

The guard trailed off as soon as he caught sight of me.

A black-cloaked knight clad in silvery armor, hand at the ready on the hilt of the Holy Thunder Sword of Caladbolg, must have struck quite the imposing figure. The guard's face went white.

Ponta was snuggled deep in Ariane's chest at the moment, unhappy at having been passed off. I didn't have much of a choice. It was hard to look intimidating with a furball on my head.

"Don't you think that's enough?" I repeated myself, lowering my voice ever so slightly. The men all stood frozen for a moment before offering a salute, followed by deep bows.

"C-certainly! I'm sorry for the trouble. We'll return to our post now."

The men made a swift exit, leaving the boy where he lay.

I hadn't expected such a reaction to my appearance. But I supposed this kind of high-class armor wasn't something just any knight would wear. They must have thought I was someone important.

I seemed to have the same effect on the crowd that had gathered around the altercation. Within a matter of moments, everyone had cleared out, retreating into the nearby buildings.

"Are you all right, boy? I can heal your injuries, if you have any."

Concern washed over the boy's face as he caught sight of me. When I knelt down next to him, he glared at me.

"I don't need nuthin' from you."

The boy held his hands to his bruised stomach as he maneuvered himself into a sitting position. He tried to stand, his face contorting in pain, but his legs just wouldn't support him.

"Please, I am...a knight of Houvan. I have the ability to use healing magic, and I can make your pain go away in the blink of an eye. What do you think?"

I pulled the black cloak tighter around me to conceal

my armor and lowered myself even more, to bring myself down to the boy's eye level. I could see a slight change in his demeanor.

"Healing...magic? You're a priest, dressed like that? Can you cure even worse injuries?"

"I am no priest, but...yes, I can."

I figured if I could bring people back from the dead, most injuries should be no problem. And even though I'd decided reviving people was mostly off limits, I didn't see the harm in healing a kid.

The boy's eyes lit up. "If you heal my sister, I'll give you some important information. Will you help?"

"Hmm. I wouldn't really feel comfortable accepting any kind of payment."

"I insist! I don't want charity from no one."

The stubborn look on the boy's face suggested he was proud beyond his years.

"What kind of information do you have?"

"Shortcuts, secret routes..." The boy's face relaxed slightly as he rattled off a list.

"Do you know a secret entrance into the castle?"

His eyes darted about to make sure no one was nearby before lowering his voice. "Why do you ask?" He looked me up and down, skeptically.

Considering how badly the guards had just roughed

him up, I doubted he was some kind of informant. I figured it wouldn't hurt to explain my situation.

"There's something in the castle that I'm looking for."

I still didn't want to risk being too specific about my objective, so I kept my answer vague. The boy furrowed his brow and glared at me in silence while he made his decision.

"Fine. I'll tell you how to sneak into the count's castle. But first, I want you to meet my sister."

"Understood. I will heal your sister, and in return you will provide me the information that I seek."

His pain seemed to have subsided, and with gritted teeth, he managed to pull himself to his feet. He started walking, albeit uneasily, down the street. Ariane and I followed him.

We were walking back along the route that had brought us here, back toward the southern gate.

The farther we got from the Houvan estate, the less glamorous the wooden houses became, replaced again with run-down hovels.

Once we reached the wall, we found ourselves in the slums, filled with rows upon rows of tiny shacks. This place was nothing like what we'd seen in other parts of town. The place reeked—some unidentifiable sourness mixed with the stench of rotting meat—suggesting that these were far from sanitary conditions. Ariane scowled from beneath her hood.

"Over here."

The boy, however, appeared unfazed by the smell. He turned down a narrow path and ducked into a shack.

The ramshackle building looked like a light breeze might blow it right over, and the roof was so low that Ariane and I had to duck to avoid hitting our heads. I had the feeling four people would be a tight fit.

Inside the hut, a little girl slept under a blanket that looked ready to fall apart at any moment. The boy shook her awake.

"Is that you, big brother...?"

Even though she referred to him as older, they didn't look all that far apart in age.

The young girl's hair was black, just like the boy's, though it was much longer and messier. She was incredibly thin, resembling a withered twig about to snap.

"What happened? Did the guards hurt you again?"

She propped herself up and focused her large, black eyes on her brother, a look of concern spreading across her face.

"This? Just a scratch. Anyway, I brought someone here who can fix your legs."

The boy wiped the blood from his mouth before glancing back to introduce his guests.

She followed his gaze and, apparently only just having taken notice of us, ducked behind her brother.

"You have nothing to fear, miss. I am not a guard nor knight of Houvan. I am Arc, a simple mercenary. This woman here is an...um, she is my travel companion. Excuse me for coming unannounced."

Ariane bowed to the girl, her cloak still pulled low over her face. Ponta's tail poked out from where the fox sat in Ariane's bosom. The little girl's expression softened slightly as soon as she saw it.

But the boy's face turned serious. He knelt, bowing low to the floor.

"Mr. Arc, can you do something about Shia's legs?"

I nodded and bid him stand up before gently pulling back the girl's blanket to take a look. Strips of wood had been wrapped around her spindly shins with thin twine.

"There's an old man here who told me that if we don't keep her like this, her legs will never heal."

I had no idea if I could cure this type of paralysis, but I hoped the mid-tier Bishop class's healing magic would be able to do the job.

I took ahold of her legs and tried to move them gently. Shia grimaced, tears forming in the corners of her eyes.

"Nnng!"

It seemed like her bones hadn't mended at all.

The boy looked up at me, fists clenched as he fought back his own tears.

"It's been a month with the splints and she hasn't gotten any better..."

It took a lot of nourishment in the early stages of recovery to heal bones. I had my doubts that she was getting what she needed from this place.

"Leave it to me. Heal!"

I waved my left hand over Shia's legs, summoning up my Bishop-tier magic skill. A warm glow enveloped her, her legs shimmering slightly before the light disappeared into her skin.

The two siblings watched in astonishment as this mystical scene unfolded before their very eyes. Ariane let out a sigh and slumped her shoulders.

I grabbed hold of Shia's legs again and moved them around to show her that they were now healed. She touched her legs in disbelief.

"They don't hurt anymore, big brother!"

"Really?"

Shia gleefully yanked the splints off her legs. She tried to stand up, but quickly had to sit back down. Her legs still wouldn't hold her weight.

"The bones are merely mended. Please, don't overburden yourself."

After having stayed in bed for nearly a month, she'd probably lost a fair amount of muscle. To make matters worse, she was so frail from malnutrition that she looked like she'd snap in two. I worried it was only a matter of time before her bones broke again.

"Boy, go get your sister something hearty to eat."

I pulled five gold coins from the leather pouch at my waist and handed them to him.

The boy's eyes went wide. However, he quickly composed himself.

"My name is Shil, and I already told you, I don't want no charity!"

"Boy...I mean, Shil. Your pride is very noble. However, I want you to think long and hard about what is most important to you before you give me your next response. Please don't think of this as charity. Rather, think of it as an opportunity for you to bring even more to the table when you return the favor. This isn't just for you, but for your sister as well."

I did my best to help him justify my meddling in his affairs, and I thought I did a pretty good job, if I say so myself.

Shil went silent for a moment. When he finally responded, the look on his face was begrudging. "Fine. But at least give me copper instead of gold. I'll stand out too much if I'm flashing around that kind of money."

He was right. I should have realized. A slum kid walking around with gold would draw a lot of unwanted attention, and possibly even be accused of stealing. In fact, if those same guards from earlier found him again, I had a feeling there'd be a repeat of this afternoon's events.

"You're really on top of things, Shil."

"Maybe you're just too careless, mister," the boy shot back, trying to cover his embarrassment at my compliment.

Ariane giggled behind me. I reached into my bag, pulled out a small leather pouch, and handed it to Shil.

The pouch was bulging with coins, and it jangled as I dropped it into Shil's small hand. His eyes bulged at the weight of it.

"How many are in here?"

"About three hundred coins, I think. You said you wanted copper, right?"

Shil looked down at the pouch in astonishment, a gasp escaping his lips. He shook his head frantically, as if holding the broken remains of a beloved toy.

"Th-this is more than enough! It should last us a long while!"

Shil stood back up, walking to a corner of the shack. He pulled a plank up from the floor and brushed away the dirt, uncovering a wooden box. If I had to guess, I'd say this was where he hid his valuables. He carefully placed the leather pouch into the box.

After returning the plank to the floor, Shil offered his thanks. He bowed his head, his eyes downcast, but I could see that he was smiling.

"I'll return the favor for this, mister. Thank you."

No matter what world you're living in, a child's smile always warms your heart.

"You've got a good big brother here, Shia."

I tousled Shil's hair and shot his sister a smile. She beamed back at me and nodded her agreement with my compliment.

Shil jerked away and immediately began rearranging his hair.

"Hey, don't treat me like a little kid!"

"You really do have a soft spot, don't you, Arc?"

There was a hint of surprise in Ariane's voice. Still, I could tell that she was smiling.

"So, about that payment you promised..."

Shil's face clouded over. I worried for a moment that maybe his story about a secret entrance had been some sort of ruse, but he stood and ushered me toward the shack's doorway.

"I'll show you the way in. Come on."

We followed Shil as he slipped between the shacks, the sun dipping below the town's walls. We finally stopped at a stone bridge that crossed a shallow river.

The bridge was covered in moss, and barely wide enough for a single horse-drawn wagon to cross it. Judging by its age, I had serious questions about how durable it was. Still, it was probably fine for us to cross on foot.

"Here it is."

Shil wasn't motioning toward the bridge, however, but rather the supports that held it up. He climbed down the embankment and beckoned for us to follow. Once under the bridge, I could see that there was a massive tunnel built into the abutment, large enough for people to walk through. A trickle of dark water poured out into the river through iron bars blocking the entrance to the tunnel.

It looked like a large sewer grate.

With practiced hands, Shil twisted several of the bars and removed them. Unfortunately, though the space he created was large enough to allow him and Ariane to slip through, for someone my size—encased in armor, no less—it was another story entirely. I got stuck on the bars as I tried to pull myself through the narrow opening.

Shil cocked his head at the ridiculous image in front of him. "Can't you take off that bulky armor?"

Wanting to get through this without revealing my teleportation magic, I grabbed another iron bar and gave it a yank.

"Nnng!"

The bar came away easily with a satisfying snap.

Shil looked at me in disbelief, but I pretended I didn't notice and started walking with Ariane down the tunnel. A little ways in, Shil pulled a lamp out of a small hollow in the wall.

This tunnel had everything. I wondered what its purpose was.

"I've got this."

Shil pulled out a striking stone, but Ariane put her finger to the lamp and chanted a quick spell.

"Fire, heed my call..."

A small flame licked out from the tip of her finger, as if she were a human lighter, and ignited the oil-soaked wick of the lamp.

Shil's eyes lit up, his voice rising an octave.

"That's amazing! You can do magic, too, lady?"

Ariane waved her hand as if it were nothing. She looked around the now-illuminated sewer.

"Does this go all the way to the castle?"

"Weeell, you'll have to walk for a while. It doesn't smell too bad here, but it gets much worse deeper in."

His response wasn't exactly encouraging. Any excitement I'd initially felt at the prospect of us being like cave explorers was quickly extinguished.

Shil led the way down the tunnel, lamp in hand, while we followed close behind. Walkways wide enough for a single person lined each side of the tunnel, so we didn't need to actually step into the sewage as we made our way deeper. The sewer reminded me somewhat of a coal mine, with its brick walls and joists running across the ceiling at regular intervals.

Shil weaved left and right down different tunnels, the stench growing stronger with every step. After an eternity, he stopped.

I looked around, but nothing about the area seemed any different from what we'd seen so far. However, Shil tapped on a brick, knocking it loose. He thrust his hand inside the hole to operate some sort of lever.

I heard a long clang followed by a loud thud as a section of the wall swung away, revealing a dark space beyond. Some sort of hidden entrance.

Shil ducked inside, lamp in hand. We followed him down a narrow staircase, which led to a damp hallway at the bottom. We walked in single file until we came to another staircase, this one heading up.

Silence hung heavy upon us. No one had said a word

since we'd entered the hidden entrance, and the sounds of our footsteps echoed noisily.

At the top of the stairs, we found ourselves in a small room with a table surrounded by several chairs. On the far side was yet another stairwell, leading up to a square panel in the ceiling.

"That stairwell will take you into the count's castle."

Shil scowled. I wasn't sure why he was making that face, but I approached the stairs all the same, running my hand along the ceiling. There was some sort of cover on the other side of the square panel built into the ceiling. Opening it would give you access to come and go freely to and from the castle. This was apparently some sort of emergency exit for people living inside. The only question was...how did it open?

Shil appeared at my side, his face pale with worry, his head bowed low.

"I'm sorry, Mister Arc! This isn't some kind of trick, I swear! You did so much for me by healing Shia's injury... I promise I'll find you a way into the castle!"

"Huh. Seems like someone placed something on top of this."

While Shil rambled, I managed to turn the panel in the ceiling, lifting both the cover and the object atop it. I poked my head through the opening, letting out a gasp of surprise.

Judging by the layers of dust, this was some kind of storage space. Its walls were painted a deep red from the dim light of the setting sun shining through the window.

"Looks like we got into the castle."

I looked down at a dumbfounded Shil, who was opening and closing his mouth in amazement, like a goldfish.

"What's wrong, Shil?"

"How did you do that, Mister Arc? It usually takes at least three grown men to lift that panel!"

The boy looked at me with all the shock of a pigeon shot by a peashooter.

"This is nothing for me."

I raised and lowered the panel a few times with one hand. His jaw dropped even farther.

"Maybe they moved things around and lightened the load a bit..."

We switched positions and Shil tried to push the ceiling panel up and out of the way, but his tiny arms couldn't budge it. While the boy busied himself trying to brute-force the panel, I turned to Ariane.

"How do you feel about sneaking into the castle after dark?"

"W-wait a minute! You actually plan on sneaking into the castle?" Shil turned to me in a panic, finally realizing what we were there to do.

I looked to Ariane, figuring she'd be better suited to field this one. She stood up from the chair she'd been sitting in.

"We need to get into the castle in order to...retrieve something inside."

She spoke with an undaunted firmness in her voice, clutching Ponta to her chest.

"J-just hold up! If you enter the castle now, it's going to cause a huge uproar!"

Seeing that Ariane and I had no intention of returning the way we'd come, Shil slid his body between us and the stairs leading up to the storage room.

Ariane faced the young boy blocking our path, her voice terse. "Uproar or not, we have a mission."

I could absolutely understand her annoyance. Shil had promised to show us the secret entrance in exchange for healing his sister's broken bones, and now he was telling us to not use it?

"Shil, if you don't tell us why you don't want us to sneak in, we'll have no choice but to continue with our original plan."

I reached up to close the ceiling cover and sat on the stairs next to the boy.

His eyes darted around, a look of uncertainty washing over him. At last, he seemed to make up his mind. He started speaking in a slow, measured tone.

"Everyone in Houvan is suffering from the hefty taxes placed on us. My mom and dad worked themselves to death just trying to pay them. The townsfolk were planning a revolt, but just before we could launch it, the Marquis du Diento was assassinated, and security became much stricter."

Ariane averted her eyes as she listened to Shil's story, a frown twisting across her face. She was the one who'd carried out the assassination that ultimately led to the extreme security measures being implemented in the town.

The count was probably worried about another elf attack. A member of the nobility engaged in the elven slave trade had been murdered. It stood to reason that another noble doing the same should be concerned.

"Apparently, they're raising taxes even higher to pay for the increased security. We learned about this entrance thanks to a sympathizer on the inside, but they haven't been able to offer us any more assistance. We're just not strong enough to rise up against the count now..."

The boy glanced up at me, as if there was something he wanted to ask but couldn't get the words out.

Obviously, if someone snuck into the castle and caused trouble, this would lead to even stricter security and possibly having the entrance blocked off entirely. Any hope of a revolt would be shattered completely.

Shil had probably been waiting for us to find out that we couldn't get past the ceiling cover so he could offer up another form of repayment. However, when he saw how easily I opened the panel, it had sent him into a panic.

If we hadn't assassinated Marquis du Diento, the revolt would already have happened. The count would probably be dead, and the enslaved elf could very well have been set free.

I looked over at Ariane, who was crouched on the floor holding Ponta.

Sure, we were responsible for this on some level, but there had to be a way we could solve both of these problems, right? My mind raced.

"Hm. What if we sneak into the count's estate while the revolt is already underway?"

If the plan was to take out the count using this secret entrance, then there shouldn't be an issue with us looking for the elves at the same time. And if we blended in with the uprising while carrying out our mission, then we wouldn't even have to worry about retribution.

"I'd be okay with that...but how soon can you organize the people to rise up?"

Ariane was back to business, arms crossed as she asked about the revolt.

If it was a month or more away, that would definitely be a problem for us.

Shil apologetically mumbled his response. "Only Rabaught would be able to answer that."

That wasn't surprising. It's not like they'd leave a kid in charge of a revolt. We'd have to get the information from the organizers themselves and then try to sell them on our idea. The odds didn't look too good.

I let out a sigh.

Shil offered to take us to this Rabaught person, the man in charge of the revolt, so we agreed. What choice did we have?

We returned the wall covering the secret entrance to its rightful place and made our way back down the sewer tunnel. By the time we reached the bridge, the sun had all but disappeared.

Shil led us back through the dimly lit streets to the slums. He brought us to a respectably built cabin...at least, respectable compared to those surrounding it. This building, unlike its neighbors, was a sturdy wooden construction sitting atop a stone foundation. Shil knocked on the door in a very particular pattern and was met with some hushed whispers.

The door opened a crack and a man eyed us suspiciously. When he saw Shil, he ushered the boy inside with his chin.

"I'll explain the situation and be right back."

Shil disappeared into the cabin.

A few moments later, Ariane and I were also allowed to enter. The man at the door glared at us as we stepped inside.

There were several more stern-looking men standing around the dimly lit room, each of them glowering in our direction. Farther inside, a large table squatted in the center of what appeared to be a dining room. A lone man sat behind it, watching us with narrowed eyes.

He looked to be around thirty, sporting a mustache and short brown hair. His well-muscled arms were covered in scars, making it clear that the man in front of us was no farmer. A bowl of wheat gruel sat in front of him. Apparently, we'd interrupted his dinner.

The man gave us a quick once-over, set his spoon down, and let out a sigh.

"Dammit, Shil! I thought I told you to let me know first before you bring guests over."

"I'm really sorry, Rabaught, but this is urgent and I—"

The man—Rabaught—cut Shil's apology off with a wave of his hand. He turned his intense gaze toward us, shooting me an odd grin.

"Arc, right? I hear you can lift heavy stones and mend broken bones. And now you're asking to use the secret entrance to the castle when we launch our revolt. But the real question is, how do I trust a man whose face I've never seen?"

Here I was, fully clad in armor, helmet firmly on my head and standing next to Ariane, whose face was also hidden, the hood of her cloak hanging low over her eyes. I had to admit, we certainly looked suspicious. Nothing I could say would change that fact. Then again, it didn't actually matter.

"We are not asking you to trust us. If you choose to ignore our request, we will simply enter the castle through the secret entrance on our own."

"What did you say?!"

Several of the stern-looking men surrounded us, murder in their eyes. However, Rabaught put up a hand to keep them at bay.

"You say that you have some sort of mission to carry out in the castle. You aren't elves, are you?"

I could feel Ariane tense slightly.

The men in the room exchanged glances, unsure of what was unfolding in front of them.

"What makes you say that?"

"According to rumor, elves were the ones responsible for Marquis du Diento's murder. Ever since then, the count has decreed that no elves are to enter Houvan."

The count was being even more cautious than I'd realized. Ariane stirred again next to me.

Rabaught crossed his arms and furrowed his brow, letting out a sigh. "It'll do me no good to try and guess who you are or why you're here. We don't have much time. Besides, you can't make an omelet without breaking a few eggs, right?"

"What do you mean, you don't have much time?"

Rabaught closed his eyes and rubbed his temples. "The first and second princes are coming up from the capital to Houvan. If we launch our revolt then, the Royal Army will have no choice but to get involved, and we'll all be put down in short order. We need to carry out our plans *before* they get here."

"Won't it still end the same way?"

Rabaught stroked his mustache. "No. If we're able to kill the count first, then other roads will open up to us. The royals have their own problems to deal with. Even if they hold an inquiry into the revolt, it will only end in my execution."

So, there was some other noble pulling the strings here. I had no idea what their plan was once they got rid of their rival—be it putting an ally in charge or taking over the town themselves—but they were clearly making a play for power.

I could only pray that whoever replaced the fallen count would treat the little folk, like Shil and Shia, better.

"In fact, we were supposed to receive backup from the capital. However, the group coming to meet us was decimated by monsters on their way here. If it weren't for that secret entrance, the revolt would already be over."

Rabaught's shoulders slumped, heavy with the burden of the situation he found himself in.

"That's quite a tragedy. When do you plan to set your plans into motion?"

"Tomorrow morning."

"That's sudden...though it works nicely for us."

"The preparations are already finished. All we need to do is give the order and our comrades in the castle will put the plan into motion. Shil will get you back to the entrance in time for the operation. You better not dawdle, boy."

Shil snapped to attention. "Aye aye!"

It looked like Ariane, Ponta, and I would have a little bit of time to kill before the uprising.

Darkness had just started to settle over the main thoroughfare running through town, though there were still a fair number of people milling about in search of food and drink—or even pleasurable company—entering the various shops lit up along the street.

Houvan served as a midway point between the Rhoden Kingdom and the Grand Duchy of Limbult, the only place where humans could engage in economic trade with the elves. This meant that elven lamps and other goods were widely used here. As such, the night was much brighter and more active than in other towns.

I walked through the busy streets for a time before stopping at one of the meat shops to buy a kebab on a bed of leaves in the shape of a boat. I also picked up a bag of boiled and salted chickpeas, which they called chana beans. I took the food back with me to Shil's hut.

"Now, which one was Shil's house..."

I'd gotten lost wandering through the twisting paths that ran through the slums.

"It's this way, Arc."

Ariane, with Ponta still clutched tightly to her, took the lead.

Given that elves were trained to keep their bearings in the forest, it was no surprise that she'd be able to do the same in a town. I was incredibly jealous of this ability. I couldn't even make it through the Umeda train station without getting lost.

"Looks like we got ourselves mixed up in something big." Ariane spoke under her breath without looking back at me.

"I know that you don't think too highly of humans, Miss Ariane. But would it really be so bad to help out Shil and his comrades?"

"Children are children, regardless of their species. Besides, this whole situation was at least partially brought about by my own actions, so I feel somewhat responsible."

Ariane looked back at me for a moment, her lips pouting slightly.

Children are children, regardless of their species... I wondered if all elves thought this way, or if it was simply her own personal philosophy. In any case, her compassion seemed to extend beyond children. After all, she'd accepted me despite the fact that I was human. Or rather, a human *skeleton*.

Speaking of which...

"Miss Ariane, do you have any misgivings about the count?"

As far as I could tell, there had been a lot of animosity between Fulish du Houvan and his subjects even before the assassination.

"Not in the least!" She scowled at me, crossing her arms.

"So, you have no stake in whether or not the count is killed in the uprising."

"That's right. We need to save the elf imprisoned in the castle. That's my only concern."

We arrived at Shil's hut and stepped inside to find him and Shia sharing a meager meal of bread scraps and dried beans.

"Shil, what happened to the money I gave you?"

He frowned at my question. "It didn't seem like a good idea to start throwing money around all of a sudden. Besides, we have enough for bread. This will be fine."

Shia nodded excitedly.

Apparently, their food situation was much more dire than I'd thought. I handed the food I'd bought earlier to the two children and gestured to Ariane to eat as well.

Shil was initially unhappy to accept such charity, but he quickly realized that his sister would need to eat something more substantial if she was to have any chance at healing. The two began stuffing their faces.

Between the meat and beans, the meal was almost entirely protein, but I figured it was far better than bread, beans, and water.

"Aren't you gonna eat, too, Mista Armor?"

The way the little girl tilted her head inquisitively made me smile. She probably hadn't had much meat in her life. Sitting next to Ponta, busily munching on the food, she looked almost like a little animal.

I ruffled Shia's hair, deciding to tell a white lie. "I ate earlier. Don't worry about me. Please, enjoy your meal."

"Gotcha!"

"Kyiii!"

Hey, Ponta, I wasn't talking to you...

Ariane shot me a glance from the corner where she sat munching on some of the chana beans. I could tell she wanted to say something, though she was staying quiet for now. Noticing the cold wind whipping through the cracks in the walls, she used her spirit magic to make a small mound of dirt with a fire on top. At least we'd be warm during the night.

We woke early the next day, the sky still dark.

The town of Houvan was quiet—the only sounds those of Shil's, Ariane's, and my footsteps as we made our way to the bridge—but I could sense a certain tension hanging in the air.

At the sewer entrance, we met two men standing as lookouts. Shil nodded to them and slipped through the space between the iron bars. Ponta, Ariane, and I followed after him.

Ariane probably could have found her way back to the storage room on her own. But I knew I needed to stick close to our guide, lest I get lost in this underground maze. I could always escape using Transport Gate if I needed to, so I wasn't actually that afraid, but still.

The hidden door was already open by the time we arrived, and there were a large number of burly, armor-clad men crowded around. The hallway was only wide enough for a single person to stand comfortably, so the men formed a line, waiting to storm the castle.

After passing through the dark, damp corridor and climbing the long staircase, we reached the small room with the panel. In the flickering lamplight, I could make out more men in leather armor crammed into the tight space, their weapons held tight, apprehension etched on their faces.

At the back of the room, we found Rabaught waiting for us at the base of the stairs leading up into the castle proper.

"You're finally here, eh? So you know, some of the soldiers who used to serve under me will be joining the uprising. Anyone wearing a white band on their arm is one of ours."

"You're an ex-soldier?"

Rabaught gave a wry smile as he stroked his mustache. "A commander, no less. And now I'm leading a revolt against the count."

Ariane's golden eyes seemed to appear out of nowhere, her charcoal cloak allowing her to slip through the shadows with ease. "What's the plan?"

"Once we're in, we'll split into two groups. The treasury is located in the courtyard between the castle's inner and outer gates. A gate team will take possession of the drawbridge and allow our allies gathering outside to enter. We've taken steps to deal with the guards outside the castle, so don't you worry about that. A group armed with these little boys here will take care of the inner gate."

Rabaught pulled a fist-sized ball from his pocket. It looked like two unglazed clay bowls held together by a string. It was slightly larger than a tennis ball.

Ariane looked surprised. "Burst Spheres, huh?"

"The lady is well informed. Yes, we'll be using these to blow the gate off its hinges. Those doors won't stand a chance."

"Aren't Burst Spheres incredibly expensive? They're basically rune stones and explosive powder."

"They were a gift from our ally in the capital. But yes, they usually cost ten gold coins each."

As far as I could gather, Burst Spheres were some type of magical hand grenade. Their co-conspirator in the capital must have been quite wealthy to send such an expensive gift. Maybe a high-ranking noble?

"Well, shall we get going?"

The tension in the room thickened as all the men turned their attention toward me. I climbed the stairwell and put my hand on the ceiling cover, swallowing hard. I pushed until I heard a heavy scraping sound and the entrance to the castle opened up.

The tension in the room turned to surprise at the sight of my strength. Rabaught let out a wry laugh and immediately began issuing orders to his men.

"No time for gawking, boys. You have jobs to do! You two, fix the door locks into place. The four of you over there, take care of anyone guarding the treasury. Shil, go get the rest of the men waiting in the tunnel."

"Yes, sir!"

Shil, now freed of his duty as a guide, turned on his heel and ran off.

Rabaught's men did as ordered and quietly made their way up the stairs into the castle.

The ceiling cover was connected by a chain to a pulley dangling from a joist in the room above. Two men worked the crank to raise the cover before shoving a large rod into the gears to fix it in place. For a moment, my hand remained where it was, making it look like I was holding nothing but air as armed men ran up the stairs past me.

We were in what appeared to be a hidden room within the stores. The wall in front of us opened out into the storeroom proper. Beyond I could see the entrance to the stores, where four men peered out into the castle through a crack in the door. One of them signaled Rabaught, who nodded in response. The men spilled silently out of the storeroom, splitting into two groups.

The group charged with taking the drawbridge moved along the base of the castle wall in a low crouch, while the archers began firing a volley at the guards patrolling atop the wall. The arrows pierced the guards' throats and heads, felling them where they stood. A second volley reduced their numbers even further. Unfortunately, one of the victims fell from the wall, hitting the ground with a loud crash.

A guard in one of the outer towers heard the noise and, with a bored yawn, slowly turned to see what it was. As soon as he spotted the group of men moving along the castle wall, we heard the high-pitched clang of an alarm bell.

Within moments, the castle sprang to life, the air suddenly full of strangled shouts and ringing steel.

The sound of men yelling and drawing weapons grew ever louder by the moment. The men making their way toward the inner gate found themselves engaged in combat with the soldiers who'd been standing guard outside. Their screams echoed across the courtyard just as the sun crested the horizon.

I watched on as one of our men, about to be slain by a guard, was saved by a soldier wearing a white armband. The guard's face displayed a mix of shock and betrayal as his comrade's sword ran him through.

Ariane and I walked through the courtyard in silence, searching for the captured elf.

I didn't exactly blend in as I walked calmly through the fray. The occasional guard would spot me and charge, but a quick smack to the head would send him tumbling to the ground unconscious.

"Explode and destroy my foes." The men charged with opening the inner gate uttered a chant as they threw their black balls toward the doors.

The roar of the explosion tore through the castle as a shower of splinters rained down upon the courtyard. Soldiers standing nearby were blown back by the shock wave and debris.

Somehow, though, the top hinges were unscathed. When the smoke cleared, the door stood firm, if leaning slightly.

Rabaught glared at the gate. "Dammit! The Burst Spheres are strong enough to break through, but we've got to get the timing perfect! Puuush! The door's already ajar, so we'll just push it open!"

The nearby rebels began pushing on the damaged door.

A man who appeared to be in charge of the defending soldiers turned issued an order. "Defend the door with your lives! Supplemental troops, fire arrows from the walls!"

I could hear men on the other side of the door yelling as they pushed back against it.

Archers prepared to rain arrows down on the invading force, but the rebels had been expecting this. Their own archers took out the new threat with ease.

The inner gate was stuck in a deadlock between two opposing forces. Rather than let the rebels waste any more time with this pointless shoving match, I ran toward the mass of men, yelling the whole way.

"Mooooove!"

They parted, clearing a path.

I charged toward the door at full speed with my shoulder out like a football player. As soon as my shoulder connected with the door, the top hinge snapped and both the door and the men supporting it were thrown back, like fallen leaves at the mercy of a stiff wind. The entrance to the castle was now wide open.

The entire courtyard fell silent for a moment, save for the distant clash of battle. Then Rabaught started issuing commands again, running toward the entrance.

"The gate's open, men! Press the attack!"

The men let out a roar as they followed their commander inside, cutting down stunned guards as they went.

Amid the chaos, I heard a loud clang followed by cheers somewhere behind us. It sounded like the first group had managed to lower the drawbridge.

The ground shook as rebels charged through the inner gate, their spirits soaring. The defenders scattered.

Absent the kind of boss or secret trick you'd expect to see when storming a castle in an RPG—neither of which seemed to be coming—it looked like the outcome of this battle was already decided.

A few enemy mages showed up to try and shoot off some sort of sorcery, but a gauntleted fist to each of their faces took them out of the battle.

"Miss Ariane, I think now would be a good time to finish our search of the castle."

"Right."

We made our way to the count's residence.

The doors to the entrance had been torn away, and invaders were already pillaging the place. Ariane furrowed her brow.

"Wasn't the point of this to rise up against a despotic ruler?"

I had to imagine that not everyone involved in the revolt was here for noble purposes. In my world, at least, this kind of looting was relatively common. Besides, we'd done the same back in Diento, so I didn't really feel like we were in a place to criticize. I did see one rebel chasing after a few chambermaids with a sword, so I punched him out.

Ariane and I moved down the hall. We'd start with the dungeon, where they usually kept prisoners.

We found a stairway leading down into the grim darkness. The guards here had apparently already abandoned their posts. There were several iron-barred cells lined up in a row, but the only people I could see were some old men and others in various states of disarray. There were no elves here.

After tearing apart several other rooms throughout the castle, we finally found the woman we were looking for in a chamber on the third floor. However, she wasn't alone.

In the center of an exquisitely decorated room stood an elven woman in a silk dress with a ball and chain tethered to her leg. In her hand, she held a bloodstained candlestick. Her green-tinged blond hair was tied back into a ponytail, revealing the characteristic pointed ears and a black metal collar around her neck. Her jade eyes were focused on two men in front of her. At her feet lay the body of a third man, blood pouring from his head.

"Hey, brother, ya think this is a real elf? I've never seen one before!"

"Shut up, ya idiot! Go get that candlestick out of her hand and get her under control! Otherwise, someone else'll come along and take her."

The two intruders advanced on the woman, apparently hoping to take her as a prize. With the chain impeding her movement, it was only a matter of time before they did.

I called out to the men. "Unfortunately, this one's been claimed. I'd like to ask you to leave."

"What the hell? You think you can just come in here and take our prize from us? You're pathetic!"

The muscular man, whom the other had called "brother," rounded on me, a heavy scowl on his face. But as soon as he saw me, his anger turned to fear. He'd probably seen me smash down the gate earlier.

I walked slowly toward the man. He drew his sword. Apparently, he didn't want to settle this with words.

I lunged, closing the distance between us, and smacked him across the temple with the back of my hand. He tumbled back, barely conscious, and collapsed in the corner.

"You bastard! Aren't you one of us?! What do you think you're doing?"

The second man—his younger brother, perhaps—

didn't show any of the fear of the first. He came straight at me, weapon raised, a wild glare in his eyes. I punched him in the face, sending him flying into the wall, his teeth scattering. He lay still.

"I helped you, but I never said I was one of you."

Ariane pulled back her hood, revealing her identity as she approached the elven woman.

"We're here to save you."

The woman's green eyes went wide at the sight of Ariane, the famous dark elf warrior.

"I didn't think anyone was coming for me... What's going on outside?"

"A revolt against the count. We're going to get you out of here. Do you know where the key is?" Ariane knelt, running her hand over the keyhole in the clasp at the woman's ankle.

"The count, the man who bought me, always has the key on him."

"Miss Ariane."

Searching for a key in a castle under attack would be a waste of time. Even if the count was still here, we couldn't be sure that he had the key on him, despite what this woman had said.

Ariane seemed to know what I was thinking. She stepped back. "Just be strong for a minute."

I grabbed the chain connecting the woman's ankle to the iron ball and pulled. The metal screeched as one of the links twisted and stretched.

"Nnnng!"

I put more strength into it, tugging at the chain, scattering pieces of metal with a loud snap.

I couldn't tell if it was a poorly made chain or simply cheap, but it couldn't handle the pressure. Either way, I was satisfied with the results.

However, we couldn't do anything about the clasp around her ankle right now. I didn't want to risk breaking her bones if I used brute force.

"We can take care of the clasp back in Lalatoya."

I discarded the remaining chain and stood.

The elf looked at me in shock, rubbing her leg. Tears poured from her eyes as she bowed her head to Ariane and me.

Ariane spoke. "Also, the mana-eater collar."

I nodded. Just as I finished removing the curse from the collar, I heard a voice from down the hall.

"Count Fulish du Houvan is dead!!!"

So, their mission had succeeded.

Cheers erupted throughout the castle, spreading outward like a wave.

Ariane and I nodded in unspoken agreement. We'd gotten what we came for. I summoned up Transport Gate, and we teleported back to Lalatoya, leaving behind the victorious townsfolk of Houvan.

SKELET☺N
KNiGHT IN
ANOTHER WORLD

CHAPTER 4

Trouble in Olav

THE NEXT DAY, Ariane and I used Transport Gate to teleport from Lalatoya back to Houvan. We used Dimensional Step to make quick jumps along the road leading to Olav, the capital of the Rhoden Kingdom.

We'd left the elf we rescued with Dillan, stayed the night, and then promptly left Lalatoya the next morning.

While we were there, I once again took the opportunity to use the bath and enjoy a delicious meal, but I knew I couldn't keep doing that forever. I was itching to get a place of my own. Constantly carrying more than a thousand gold coins on me only added to that desire.

Glenys had told me I could come by their place any time, but obviously she didn't mean *literally* any time. She'd also added a condition: If I came by, I needed to bring Ponta with me. The little furball was incredibly popular with women and children.

Currently, Ponta sat in its rightful spot atop my helmet, letting out little yawns as the scenery changed from one teleport to the next.

The trip from Houvan to the capital normally took around two days by cart, but we could do it in just half a day using Dimensional Step. Since the land was practically flat the entire way—mostly fields, with the occasional farm or village—I had a great line of sight, allowing me to teleport long distances.

However, since this route ran straight to the capital, there was also a lot of traffic. I had to choose teleportation spots that were a little off the road and not easy to spot.

We soon came to a large river running north to south—the Lydel. The way the light reflected off the surface of the water reminded me of a silver serpent slithering through the fields.

A massive bridge spanned the river. On the far side, I could see the rounded walls—four layers deep—of an enormous city. Even from here, I could tell that the place was immense.

It was the first time I'd seen anything even approaching the scale of this city. Given how few artificial structures there were in this world, it was hard for me to describe this...monument to human achievement.

The words just slipped out of my mouth. "It's...stunning."

Ariane looked quizzically over at me. I just shook my head in response.

With the capital in sight, we made our way back to the road and blended into the crowd of travelers.

We'd come to Olav to gather information for our future missions. After all, it was the largest concentration of people in the whole kingdom. There were two more names on the elf purchase contracts: Lundes du Lamburt and Drassos du Barysimon, probably both men.

Even from a distance, we could easily see all of the people and carts crossing the bridge. Like the bridge in Diento, this one led straight into the capital itself. Unlike Diento, Olav contained a whole city between its third and fourth walls alone.

We crossed the bridge and found ourselves at the east gate. The walls stood at least thirty meters tall, though they looked even more massive against the surrounding plains, differing from Lalatoya, which was ringed with trees. The gate itself was about ten meters wide, allowing for crushing numbers of people and carts to come and go unimpeded. The whole scene screamed of prosperity.

There was one line for carts and another for people. Wave after wave of each were swallowed by the city as they made their way inside. Ariane joined the line for people. When we reached the front, a guard stopped us. He looked us both over quickly, but didn't show any sort of reaction. He sounded annoyed, speaking in a flat, business-like tone as he repeated the same phrase he'd been saying all day:

"I need your papers, or it'll be one sek per person to enter."

I handed over two silver coins. The guard gestured toward the entrance with his chin and moved on to the next person in line. As we passed through the east gate, I had to crane my neck just to see the top of it.

We were now in Olav, the capital of the Rhoden Kingdom.

The gate opened out into a huge market, shops lining both sides of a stone road as wide as the gate that stretched all the way to the next wall. The market was filled with bustling crowds milling about the shops. The people were dressed in all manner of clothes, further adding to the excitement of the capital—the flower of the kingdom.

Ponta's neck turned this way and that as it tried to take in all the new sights.

But I knew, as beautiful as Olav might be, any city

with a population of this size was bound to have problems. It was just like they used to say: "Fights and fires are the flowers of Edo." Up the road, I could already see a quarrel breaking out.

Two rough-looking, muscular men faced off against a single man. As far as I could tell, the two men were the instigators. The man wore wrapped cloth around his head and face, leaving only his eyes uncovered. Standing at over two meters tall—a whole head taller than even me—he easily stuck out from the crowd. The upper half of his body was bare, revealing a bronze, well-toned chest. He wore a cloak that hung from his shoulders like a cape.

Even from a distance, I could tell that there was something strange about this large man. He looked like some sort of conqueror from another century...and he gave the impression that he believed he was one, too.

"Whaddya doin' showin' your giant face around here, ya pufferfish?!"

The smaller man's attempt to show how tough he was in front of the turbaned time traveler came off as pathetic more than anything else. It was probably an unspoken rule among thugs that you had to be taken seriously in an argument.

The man in the turban looked back at him as if he were a non-threatening animal, trying to continue on his way.

"Don't ignore me, ya moron!"

Some of the other men standing around drew daggers, howling as they closed in on the man.

I heard a cry from within the crowd of watching rubberneckers at the sight of bladed weapons. The circle of people backed away to give the combatants more space.

The next sound I heard was a cry of pain from two of the thugs rushing toward the turbaned man. Right as they'd closed in, the man had their heads, one in each hand, and lifted them into the air.

"Gyaaaaagh! My head! My head!"

"Cut it out! Stoppit!"

The men cried like babies, thrashing about, but the turbaned man only tightened his grip.

The roaring crowd went silent at the terrifying show of strength. I could almost hear the men's skulls starting to crack through the unnatural silence.

"Hey, what do you think you're doing over there?!"

Several guards, having heard the commotion, broke through the onlookers. As soon as they appeared, the crowd dispersed like newly hatched spiders. When I turned my attention back to the fight, to my surprise, the time-traveling man had vanished. The two thugs lay on the ground, unconscious and with an awful mess between their legs.

Ariane let out a sigh as the stench washed over us, scowling under her cloak. "What a barbarous place..."

"All the easier for us to fade into the crowd."

Ariane and I sped away from the scene of the incident as we spoke, weaving our way down the street and avoiding guards.

"First, we need to find a place to stay. Then we can split up to start gathering information."

Ariane nodded in agreement, though she seemed displeased with all the people. "You're probably right."

After we'd walked a ways down the main thoroughfare, I stopped a young man to ask for directions.

"Excuse me, but could you tell me where I can find an inn?"

The man's eyes went wide when he saw me, and he stumbled over his words. "Huh? I, umm, well...an inn, yes. For a knight like yourself, I think you'll want to go to the second district."

According to the young man, we were in the fourth district, where the commoners lived. The closer we got to the palace, the higher the class and wealth of the people who lived there. The first district was reserved for nobles, and it was apparently quite rare for a normal person to pass beyond the wall closest to the palace.

I offered the young man my thanks and a silver coin

before Ariane and I resumed walking. The road from the east gate led all the way to the second district. We continued until we arrived at the third wall's gate.

The third wall was only around twenty meters tall, though it was still quite impressive. Various stalls ran along it, giving the whole place a kind of old-town feeling. Two guards stood on either side of the third wall's gate, though we didn't need to pass any type of inspection. The mood was considerably calmer on the far side of the wall, but there was still a certain liveliness due to the sheer volume of people. The wooden houses of the fourth district gave way to slightly more stylish stone houses.

Despite what the young man had said, I worried we'd stand out if we went into any higher-class areas, so we decided to find an inn here in the third district.

Breaking off from the main thoroughfare, we took a side road away from all of the shops that followed a large waterway running behind them. Gondola-like boats, filled with people and packages, meandered back and forth under stone bridges that led to the vast residential district beyond. The whole scene looked a bit like Venice.

We saw inns, bars, and restaurants as we made our way along the busy street. It was nowhere near as packed as the main thoroughfare, but it was still full of people.

"That inn looks like it could be nice." Ariane pointed to a quaint three-story building up ahead.

We entered and reserved two rooms, though we opted to continue our walk through the city rather than turning in just yet. Now that our accommodations were figured out, it was time to gather information. Ariane and I split off in front of the inn.

Since this city was far larger than any I'd been to thus far, I decided to stick to the roads that ran parallel to the main thoroughfare to keep from getting lost. I didn't anticipate finding anything of note if I went down the alleys anyway. At least, that's what I told myself.

I hope it wouldn't be too hard to locate the information we were looking for. After all, Fulish du Houvan had lived in a town bearing his own name. Maybe all I needed to do was look for towns named Lamburt and Barysimon.

I decided to ask the person who would know best—a merchant. I thought back to the route we'd taken to the inn, and returned to the stalls lining the third wall of the city. Merchants peddling everything from produce to perfume cried out toward the townspeople as they hurried past.

Many of the stalls here were selling fruits and vegetables, which Ponta eyed intently from its perch atop my head. I could feel its tail wagging through the helmet.

One stall in particular caught the fox's attention.

"Kyiii!"

An old man was selling dried berries in bulk from a large barrel. Ponta's nose caught a whiff of their sweet scent and fell into an excited frenzy.

"Excuse me, sir. I'd like to purchase two cups of your berries. You can pour them right in here."

I pulled out a small leather pouch and handed it to the old man.

"Ah, absolutely, Sir Knight."

The old man moved slowly as he scooped some dried berries and deposited them in my pouch.

"By the way, you don't happen to know of anywhere nearby—a property, or possibly a town—by the name of Lamburt or Barysimon, do you?"

The man, measuring cup still in hand, cocked his head in thought. After a moment, he nodded emphatically, as if he had just remembered something.

"Yes, I know of Lamburt. There's a port city to the west of the capital by that name."

"Oh? And how far west is it?"

He set the cup down on the barrel and crossed his arms. "Hmm...I'd say it's about a six-day trip by carriage, perhaps?"

Six days by carriage... That was quite a distance.

"And how about Barysimon?"

The man shook his head. "Nope. Never heard of it."

"Ah, well, thank you for your time, kind sir. Here, for your trouble."

I took the two scoops of dried berries and handed the old man five silver coins.

The man's eyes went wide for a moment, then he composed himself, flashing me a toothy smile... Well, he flashed me the few teeth he had left.

I went from stall to stall, asking the owners if they recognized the name Barysimon, feeding the dried berries to Ponta as I inquired. But no one had heard of the name. I was starting to wonder if I was going about this all wrong—despite having gotten a good lead on Lamburt—when a monotone voice called out to me from behind.

It was a girl's voice. One I'd heard before.

"Well, it's been awhile."

I turned around, looking down. Somewhere in the back of my mind, I knew I'd met this person before.

The girl's azure-colored eyes regarded me from under her oversized hat. Her black hair was cut short, and she was dressed in all black, the clothes fitted to her form for easy movement. I figured she couldn't be more than 150 centimeters tall.

She wore a gauntlet and shin guards, and carried a short sword on her lower back. She didn't look like she was from around here.

The girl's gaze slowly drifted up to the top of my head, where Ponta was sitting, then she pulled her eyes down to look directly at me.

I frantically searched my memory for any recollection of those deep, azure eyes. "So, I know we've met before, but..."

"I'm glad you were able to pull things off so well in Diento." The girl spoke in a flat voice, her eyes never wavering. Suddenly it hit me—an image of a cat ninja in the marquis' castle.

"Oh! You're that ninja girl from before!"

Her narrow eyebrows twitched in response. "Ninja...? So I *did* hear right last time." The girl stood at stiff attention. "I'd like to speak with you about something. Do you have time?"

I nodded—what else could I do in the face of that intense gaze?—and she motioned for me to follow her down an empty side street.

Once we were away from the bustle and she'd assured herself there was no one nearby, she seemed to relax slightly.

"Sorry for not introducing myself earlier. My name is Chiyome, and I'm one of the six members of the Sword and Spirit Jinshin clan."

Her name had a Japanese ring to it, but the I wasn't familiar with the other word she'd used.

"Jinshin clan?"

"'Jin' for 'sword' and 'shin' as in 'heart.' It means a person who can endure challenges." No matter how you put it, the name had a very ninja-esque feel to it.

While I was busy thinking all this over, the young girl in front of me looked back at me with her deep azure eyes and gestured for me to introduce myself. "And you are...?"

"Sorry! My name is Arc. I am a traveler. Circumstances have brought me to wander the lands."

"I see. So, Mister Arc, why do you call me a ninja?"

She looked back at me attentively, intent on not missing a single word in my response. The way she spoke implied that she knew what a ninja was, though it seemed highly unlikely that she'd been drawn in from another world like I had.

I watched her face closely as I responded, looking for some sort of clue.

"Well, in my country, there are spies who dress similarly to you. We refer to them as ninja."

She closed her eyes briefly, seemingly satisfied with my response. "Hmm, I see. 'Ninja' is a secret name known only to our clan, so I suppose you must be from the same country as our great founder."

That meant that the great founder was probably Japanese like me, or at least a person from Earth who was familiar with the ninja.

"How many generations has it been since the founder came along?"

"Hmm...the current head of the clan is the twenty-second in line since the great founder gave their teachings."

I'd expected something like this, but twenty-two generations meant that there was definitely no way the founder was still alive. Still...what was the harm in asking?

"And has this great founder already passed on?"

"Yes. Six hundred years ago, the great founder saved some of the cat people and brought them together to form a new clan, the Jinshin clan."

"Why are you telling me all this?"

Ariane's father, Dillan, had told me that the beastmen had all been oppressed, and even enslaved. And yet here was this girl in a human city—the capital, no less—wearing a disguise and talking about her clan. I had to imagine it was dangerous for her here.

As if that behavior wasn't daring enough, her reply took it a step further. "I'd like to ask for your help."

Given what she'd been up to in Diento, I had a pretty good guess as to what that job might be—freeing the mountain people held captive in the capital. Yet it seemed strange for her to ask me, a human, to help save her comrades from their human oppressors.

"Miss Chiyome, would your clan be okay with you asking *me* for help?"

She nodded.

She must have had some sort of plan, but I was already helping Ariane, so I couldn't agree without giving it some thought.

"I'm currently assisting an elf with another matter. I'm afraid I'm in no position to help you out at this time."

Chiyome stood there, deep in thought, before responding. "Then allow me to meet this elf. If they will agree to you helping me, then I will provide you with information in return." There was an adversarial note to her normal monotone.

"And what would that information be?"

Her dark azure eyes stared straight into me. "You're looking for the people named on those purchase contracts, aren't you?"

"That's true... However, we've already identified two of the three people."

"I see... So that just leaves Drassos du Barysimon." The young girl responded matter-of-factly.

"If you know that much, then I assume you know the whereabouts of this person?"

"Of course."

She was living up to her identity as a ninja.

Obviously, I wanted the information, but I could only get it by helping her free the slaves.

I had no qualms about helping her, but I was hesitant to do anything in the capital that might draw a lot of attention. If I became wanted, that would make it much harder to travel.

Still, as soon as I'd told her that we'd already uncovered two of the three people listed on the purchase contracts, she was able to name Barysimon. Did that mean that he would be the hardest to find? If so, then it seemed unlikely that simply asking around town would get us anywhere. On the contrary, word might spread that some suspicious people were looking for a person by that name.

Dillan had mentioned that Chiyome's people were descended from spies. It was only natural that they'd be good at getting their hands on information.

"I'd like to talk this over with my partner."

"Then take me with you. I can speak with your partner directly."

She might have looked like a child, but her intense, unwavering eyes suggested otherwise. Still, it seemed unlikely that she might actually want to harm Ariane if I brought her along.

"Understood. Please follow me, Miss Chiyome."

I made my way back to the main thoroughfare, passing through the gate at the third wall with Chiyome in tow. She might have been small, but she had no problem keeping up.

Ponta, apparently bored from the long conversation, had fallen asleep atop my helmet. As we walked, I occasionally had to reach up to keep the fox from falling off.

We entered the inn and made our way to the third floor, where I motioned for Chiyome to enter one of our rooms. I bid her sit in one of the chairs while I sat on the bed. Ponta woke and began testing the firmness of the mattress with its front paws.

The room grew silent, an odd tension filling the void between me and Chiyome. The ninja girl fidgeted slightly in the chair as she watched Ponta and me.

"Miss Chiyome, the toilet is down on the first floor."

"I don't need it!"

I'd only said this to ease the tension, but her face had flushed at my suggestion. She was quite the proper young lady.

I reached into my bag and handed her my leather pouch.

Chiyome looked at me quizzically. She poured the contents of the pouch into her palm, and Ponta immediately lifted its head.

"Apologies for not making the introductions sooner. This is Ponta, a cottontail fox. Nuts and fruits are some of its favorite foods."

Chiyome looked down at the dried berries in her hand and then back at the slowly approaching spirit creature. The corners of her mouth relaxed into a grin.

Ponta had reached her feet and was now moving back and forth eagerly, staring up at the dried berries. It wasn't yet comfortable enough to jump onto Chiyome's lap, but that was likely only a matter of time.

Chiyome stretched out her hand and Ponta cautiously approached, its excitement evident in the way its tail twitched from side to side. The ninja girl's eyes lit up and she let out a laugh as Ponta started munching on the fruits.

"I was surprised to see a spirit creature bonded to a human like you, Mister Arc." Chiyome petted Ponta with one hand while continuing to feed it berries with the other.

I let out a wry laugh. "Everyone says that."

Chiyome shook her head. "No, I mean that spirit animals can sense humans' ill intentions. You must be quite trustworthy for it to feel this comfortable with you."

I looked back down at Ponta, only to find that the fox had jumped onto Chiyome's lap, begging for more berries.

If what she said was true, then that would make me something like Ponta's safety blanket. I decided to not think too much about it.

"I've been wondering...how did you know I was there to save the elves when we first met?" Most people would assume a knight showing up in such a place was a slave trader rather than a rescuer.

Chiyome looked up at me.

"Elves, humans, beastmen...we all have our own unique scents. Not only were you accompanied by a spirit animal, but I picked up the scent of elves on you. However..."

She trailed off for a moment. "There was something else about your smell...your aura that was different, Mister Arc. I've never felt anything like it."

Being made entirely of bones, I couldn't imagine what might actually give off such a smell.

Her blue irises narrowed in on me, as if she were looking straight into my helmet. Did she know my secret? Could she tell? Or was I just being paranoid?

The room had fallen back into silence by the time there came a knock at the door.

There weren't many people who would be stopping by this room, so I invited the person on the other side to come in. A moment later, a person in a familiar charcoal gray cloak stepped inside. Their eyes immediately locked on to Chiyome, still seated in her chair, feeding Ponta dried berries.

They regarded each other for a moment before Ariane slowly removed her cloak, exposing her amethyst-colored skin and pointed ears. Chiyome took off her oversized hat, her own twitching cat ears poking up out of her black hair.

"Introductions are in order. Miss Chiyome, this is Miss Ariane, my elf partner."

Ariane bowed slightly, narrowing her golden eyes as she shot me a questioning look.

"Miss Ariane, this is Miss Chiyome of the Jinshin clan. She was the one in Diento who gave me the seventh contract."

"Nice to meet you, Miss Ariane. I am Chiyome."

Chiyome set Ponta on the floor, stood up, and offered her right hand to Ariane. Her black ears twitched, as if they were searching for something.

Ariane took her hand and shook it. "I am Ariane Glenys Maple. Thank you for providing us with the information."

"A knight of Maple... The most elite warriors in the entire Great Forest of Canada, I hear." Chiyome returned the handshake, her azure eyes filled with wonder.

So, the ninja clan was at least somewhat familiar with the elves. Ariane looked slightly surprised.

"Well, would someone like to tell me why little Chiyome is here in your room?" Ariane placed her hands on her waist, alternating her gaze between Chiyome and me.

Chiyome might have been a child, but her behavior was anything but. It seemed more than a little strange to refer to her as "little Chiyome." Still, the ninja girl didn't seem bothered by it.

Actually, when I looked closer, I could see her tail swishing and ears twitching. She might have even liked it.

"Before we get into that, I'd like to hear what information you found, Miss Ariane."

If she'd discovered the whereabouts of Barysimon, that would change everything.

She looked back at me quizzically, her eyebrows furrowing.

"I didn't find out anything. Even in this cloak, I still seemed to attract the weirdest men as I walked around town." She punctuated this complaint with a heavy sigh, the exhaustion apparent on her face. I could easily imagine her magnificent chest serving as an alluring flame to the "moths" known as men. I didn't recall her having any such problems when we were out together. I supposed my presence served as a type of insect repellant.

"That's unfortunate. I was able to learn about one of the two names, Lamburt. The other, however..."

Chiyome stepped forward. "Allow me to continue."

She recapped the conversation she and I had earlier, a cool look on her face the whole time. Ariane closed her eyes as she listened to the story.

As soon as Chiyome finished, Ariane responded.

"I don't mind. I know what it's like to have your comrades hunted as slaves." She kept her voice low, the anger in it apparent.

Chiyome looked surprised.

I was surprised as well. Though it was admirable for Ariane to put her own needs aside, I couldn't help but wonder why she would so easily agree to something like this. Chiyome and the other mountain people—beastmen, as the humans called them—didn't have a treaty to protect them like the elves did. There was no law that prevented humans from keeping them as slaves. They had no rights, just like animals. Worse, in this world, there weren't even any animal cruelty laws.

"You don't need to get involved in this, Arc," Ariane said. "You only agreed to help me, after all." She brushed back her snow-white hair, blinked her long-lashed eyelids, and turned her golden gaze on me. There was a deep sorrow in her expression.

Chiyome's cat ears moved almost imperceptibly.

"Of course I'll help, but I think it would be best to keep a low profile."

I said this primarily for my own benefit, of course, but if it came out that elves were involved in this rescue, it would become even harder for Ariane to travel around. After all, the increase in security throughout Houvan had resulted in a revolution.

This seemed to strike a chord with Ariane, who furrowed her brow. "What kind of help did you have in mind, exactly?"

Chiyome cleared her throat. "We plan to attack the largest slave trading house in Olav."

So, they were going the route that would draw the most attention. And as if that wasn't enough, Chiyome said that the attack on the slave house was merely a diversion.

I was having a hard time believing that they'd recruit outside help for such a dangerous mission. I struggled to keep my tone steady. "Miss Chiyome, what do you mean by 'diversion'?"

Ariane leaned in close, listening intently as well.

"Exactly what it sounds like. The Etzat Market has strong ties to the government. The moment it's under attack, guards will descend upon it. The Royal Army might even respond."

"Doesn't that mean that all of your newly freed allies will be swarmed by soldiers?"

Ariane frowned, seeming to share my concern.

"We'll free our allies being held in the Etzat Market, but they won't be able to run for long. However, in the ensuing chaos, we're going to attack four other locations where our comrades are being held. They should be able to escape in all the confusion."

"So, you'd use your own comrades as a decoy so that others can go free?" I was surprised at the harshness in my tone.

Chiyome's azure eyes wavered. "We can't save everyone. If ten have to die for a hundred to live, then so be it."

Chiyome couldn't have been more than thirteen or fourteen. She had to be struggling with the idea of sacrificing her own comrades. However, she held her head up high, choosing to stay strong in the face of everything.

Without thinking, I placed my hand on her small head, gently brushing back her soft, black hair. Down at her feet, Ponta weaved between her legs, using the soft fur along its neck to try to comfort her.

Chiyome looked up at me with her clear, azure eyes. I couldn't really say why, but I just wanted to see her smile. If there was anything I could do to help this girl who'd come all the way to the land of humans, then I'd do it gladly.

I imagined myself spending more time in the elven villages and even living among the mountain people. There were whole fandoms in Japan who'd love to be in such a position.

Ariane turned her gaze toward me. I could tell what she wanted without her even needing to say anything.

I nodded and looked around my room, burning the image into my mind.

"Transport Gate!"

A bluish-white pillar of light rose around us, Ariane, Chiyome, and I standing still while Ponta rolled around excitedly.

Chiyome looked up to me, her surprise evident on her face. The next moment, we were in the middle of a grassy clearing, a large boulder with a tree wrapped around it sitting in front of us. A bed and chair sat in the middle of the clearing as well, looking incredibly out of place. Apparently, Transport Gate's area of effect had grabbed the furniture in the room along with us.

Chiyome's head jerked back and forth, the ears atop her head twitching frantically as she tried to grasp what had just happened.

Ariane made a face and let out a low groan, evidently not having expected to teleport all of a sudden like that.

Maybe I'd misunderstood the look she gave me?

I'd wanted to show off Transport Gate to Chiyome, since it could be useful to our upcoming operation.

Chiyome finally came back to herself, though she was still at a loss for words. "Wh-where are we?"

"We're in the forest at the base of the Anetto Mountains."

Chiyome continued to pivot her head back and forth, muttering to herself. "The Anetto Mountains...huh. So, you can also use space-time ninjutsu abilities?"

"Space-time...ninjutsu?"

"According to the legends, the great founder, Master Hanzo, mastered the technique known as space-time ninjutsu, allowing him to travel great distances instantaneously. You can use it too, Mister Arc?"

It wasn't ninjutsu, really. Just simple teleportation magic. Nor was space-time ninjutsu one of the skills I'd learned from the top-tier Ninja class. But as usual, there was no guarantee that the world here was a one-to-one match with the game. It was possible that teleportation magic was simply known as space-time ninjutsu to the beastmen. And with a name like Hanzo, the great founder must have been quite the ninja maniac.

I finally asked what was on my mind. "Miss Chiyome... is that your real name?"

Chiyome puffed out her chest and beamed with pride.

"No. My name is one of six passed down to the most powerful ninja in the clan."

That meant that her name came from Mochizuki Chiyome, a famous female ninja from my world. If there were six in total, then I had to imagine the others had names like Kirikagure Saizo and Sarutobi Sasuke.

Ariane's voice brought me back to reality. "Why don't we at least go back to the inn to discuss the next steps?"

She was right. The forest was full of monsters and other dangers. Not that such things would be a problem for a group as well trained as ours, but it wasn't exactly an environment suited for strategizing.

I summoned up the spell again and brought to mind the image of our room at the inn. The spreading magic pillar glowed even brighter than before, and, in a flash, we were back in the room...along with the bed and chair.

Ponta patted the floor with its front paws, as if to confirm that the grassy meadow had been replaced with hardwood.

"Kyii?"

Chiyome also looked impressed as she glanced around the room.

"Since Arc will also be helping you out, that means we'll have access to teleportation magic..." Ariane's voice trailed off, an inquisitive look on her face as she shot me a glance. She then turned her gaze toward Chiyome. After all, the young ninja girl was the only one who actually knew when this operation would be carried out.

"That was magic? Well, if we can use that..." Chiyome crossed her arms and muttered to herself, as if examining how this changed her plans. "Mister Arc, how far can your magic take you?"

"I can teleport to any unique location that I've been to in the past."

Transport Gate wasn't restricted by distance. Even if I were surrounded inside a building, I could use the spell to teleport somewhere safe and far away...meaning, for example, that I could draw out enemies and then make an easy escape.

Chiyome asked several follow-up questions about how many people I could take, how frequently I could use the spell, and so on. However, I could only give my best guess on many of these, since there was still a lot that I didn't know myself.

Based on the game, I could probably use Transport Gate a hundred times or more without issue. Besides, I'd had no problem using Rejuvenation over and over, and that consumed far more magic than Transport Gate.

After hearing my explanation of how teleportation magic worked, Chiyome grew excited.

She and Ariane started putting together a plan of attack for the slave market, though it was still very similar to the original plan—they would lay siege to the market along with their freed comrades.

"Mister Arc, Miss Ariane, I should probably go tell my allies of the change in plans. Please continue the preparations while I'm away." Chiyome hopped out the window, running off along the rooftops.

"Miss Ariane, did you get the impression that we're carrying out the operation tonight?"

"That's how it sounded to me."

I looked out the window, but Chiyome had disappeared.

"Well, I guess we'd best prepare as much as we can."

Ariane shot me a quizzical look. "But what should we prepare, exactly?"

I stuck my index finger in the air and struck a confident pose. "We'll need to disguise ourselves, of course."

I was actually being quite serious, but Ariane just stared at me blankly.

"But...you're already wearing a helmet. That should be enough, no?"

If looks could kill, this one would have at least maimed me. I'd given this plan a lot of thought. I felt as though my eyes were welling up with tears. But of course, skeletons can't cry.

I typically covered my flashy armor with my Twilight Cloak, but that still left my head exposed. I'd definitely stand out among the members of the raiding party. Even if the plan went off without a hitch, I'd have a pretty hard time moving around human towns if there was a follow-up investigation involving my helmet.

Of course, the same was true for the other times we'd snuck into various estates, but this time we were dealing with nobles and slave traders who *weren't* violating any treaties. They weren't criminals, at least in the eyes of the law. Though they might be capturing mountain people, we would still just be attacking a slave house operating on the up and up under human law. Being nothing more than an insurgent, it seemed like a wise idea to exercise some caution and disguise myself in the event that someone came looking for us afterward.

"Well, at least I don't need anything. See? I'm fine like this." Ariane tugged her charcoal cloak low over her face again.

It seemed like I'd managed to sell her on the idea that *I* needed a disguise, but she had no intention of getting one for herself.

That was the end of that, so I left Ariane behind and headed out alone to find my new look. Once again, I made my way toward the stalls lining the third wall.

A stall selling some strange items caught my eye.

Numerous traditionally handcrafted goods were spread out across a cloth-covered table, ranging from disturbing statuettes of animals, to tools with undiscernible uses, to some bizarre-looking masks that I could only assume were for festivals.

A man with a wide grin—the stall owner, I assumed—approached me as soon as I stopped to look.

"Hello there, good sir! Do you see anything that interests you?"

The man's round chin was covered in a thin beard, and he was wearing a gaudy, multi-colored coat. There was something slimy about the way he called out to me, rubbing his hands together the whole while.

I picked up one of the masks. It was made of wood, painted black, and carved into the shape of a human face. The eyes gave off a vacant stare, and the mouth sported a creepy grin, almost as if it had been torn into that shape. The back of the mask was decorated with feathers, providing coverage for your whole head.

The stall owner wasted no time swooping in to close the sale.

"Ah, I can see that you have good taste, sir. This comes from the nomads living in the untamed wastes far beyond the border of the East Revlon Empire. Magicians with special abilities known as 'Soodu' wear the masks during their rituals. It's incredibly rare."

I continued to look the mask over as he spoke, the devious look never quite leaving his face. I was actually was fond of the design, and I'd be able to wear it over my helmet.

"How much?"

The stall owner grinned. "Well, considering its incredible rarity, I've priced it at twenty sok."

Twenty gold coins. I set the mask down and started to walk away, but the seller hurried over and called me back.

"A joke! It was merely a joke, good sir! Fifteen sok? How does that sound?"

"Ten sok," I countered.

Sweat ran down the man's neck as we continued to negotiate, his smile slowly fading. Ultimately, we settled on thirteen sok.

For a normal person, thirteen gold coins might have seemed absurd for a hand-carved wooden mask. However, there was something about the mask that changed its value entirely for me. I liked it so much that I would have been fine paying the original twenty sok, though I didn't like the idea of paying a man like this exactly what he was asking.

I handed over the money and put the mask into my bag. I'd gotten what I was looking for. All that was left was to talk with Chiyome, the only person who had the full picture of the upcoming operation.

The palace sat at the very center of Olav, the capital of the Rhoden Kingdom. Off in a secluded room, a lone magical lamp provided illumination as the sun sank outside. The light reflected off a silver cup as a man threw it across the room, a vein bulging in his neck.

The cup hit the ground, rolling into the corner with a clang that reverberated throughout the room. The wine inside splashed everywhere, filling the air with a fruity aroma. The two other men in the room watched the cup's journey before returning their attention to the enraged man.

"Dammit! Why did they have to kill Count du Houvan now, of all times?!"

The man stood up from a leather sofa and clenched his now-empty fist. Dakares Ciciay Karlon Rhoden Vetran, the second prince of the Rhoden Kingdom, ran his hands through his hair and breathed rapidly, his face contorted, his blue eyes burning with rage.

"The townsfolk rose up in revolt. We've been unable to reach the count through the chaos." One of the men, the target of Prince Dakares' intense stare, spoke slowly as he repeated the report from his messenger.

The man's name was Duke Maldoira du Olsterio, one of the seven dukes of Rhoden and general of the Third Royal Army. He was an older man with graying brown hair and a well-groomed mustache, and he was far more muscular than his years might suggest.

Prince Dakares continued his tirade, this time directed at the monsters. "If those haunted wolves hadn't shown up, Sekt would've been finished by now!"

The man next to General Maldoira spoke up, attempting to placate the prince. "Your Highness, if the monsters hadn't appeared along the route, we would have arrived in Houvan as planned and been caught in middle of the revolt."

Cetrion du Olsterio, a brawny man wearing a lieutenant general's uniform, looked like a younger copy of General Maldoira.

Unfortunately, Cetrion's words only served to further enrage the prince.

"You're trying to put a positive spin on this?! We could have taken advantage of the chaos to murder Sekt!"

The two men could do nothing but sigh in response to the prince's foul mood.

They had plotted with Count du Houvan to murder

Prince Sekt, but the sudden appearance of monsters along the route to Houvan had prevented them from arriving in time, and their co-conspirator had ended up dead at the hands of his own subjects.

"The timing was wrong, nothing more. We need to keep an eye out for the next opportunity."

General Maldoira provided the rest of his report, frustration clear in his voice. A contingent of the Royal Army stationed in the capital had been dispatched to secure the roads and pacify the situation in Houvan. For now, it would be difficult for Dakares' men to leave the capital, meaning that the trip to Houvan had to be called off.

The prince muttered angrily to himself. "And that hag Yuriarna managed to slip through my fingers! I hear she's reached Limbult..."

Someone knocked loudly on the door. "Master Maldoira, I have an urgent matter that needs your attention!"

Cetrion moved to the door, opening it a crack. The soldier offered a swift salute before whispering his news into the lieutenant general's ear. Cetrion nodded, then sent the messenger on his way. He repeated the report to his father in a low voice.

Prince Dakares glared at the two men, making no effort to conceal the annoyance in his voice. "What is it?"

Maldoira cleared his throat. "Apparently, the Etzat Market's central office is under siege. The attackers are quite skilled, and the market is asking for emergency assistance from the army. What should we do?"

The prince rubbed at his temples. "If it's not one thing, it's another!"

The Etzat Market was used heavily by the major trading companies—not to mention elven slavers—so Dakares was in no position to deny a request from the market's chairman.

The prince let out a curse-laden scream. After catching his breath, he turned his steely gaze to the general.

"I'll smooth things over with Father later. Assemble a squad and suppress the attack. The chairman will owe us a heavy debt if the general himself is involved."

Prince Dakares's lips twisted into a smile, eliciting a grin from Cetrion as well.

"Understood."

The general bowed to the prince before striding out of the room.

After his father was gone, Cetrion spoke up. "We haven't been able to confirm it yet, but we've received a report that elves might have been involved in the Houvan incident."

"What?!" The prince glowered at Cetrion.

"This attack on the Etzat Market might also be their doing."

"How do you mean?" A tinge of anxiety had entered the prince's voice.

"According to the reports, Marquis du Diento had been keeping an elf who has since disappeared. Count du Houvan had also purchased an elf. It seems likely that these two incidents are related." Cetrion struggled to keep the tone of his voice even.

"Are you suggesting that now they're after me, the one pulling the strings? No, no...that would be silly. Whoever's behind this, there's no way they could breach the royal palace."

"It's possible that this is the work of someone *within* the nobility. Marquis du Diento's castle was an imposing fortress, and you can see how well that worked out for him. If the attack on the market is merely a distraction, then someone might be coming to take your life as we speak."

"So, what are you saying?"

"I think it would be best to lay low, somewhere no one would think to look for you. I've already prepared a place in the first district. Please, come with me, Your Highness."

Prince Dakares hesitated for a moment, then nodded in agreement. Cetrion went to the door and spoke in a low voice to a messenger he had standing by.

"Prepare a carriage at the rear entrance for the prince. Hurry!"

The lieutenant general summoned several guards to escort the prince. This hallway was reserved only for the royal family, their relatives, and closest associates, so the only sound was that of their hurried footfalls echoing through the empty halls.

When they arrived at the rear entrance, a black carriage bearing the crest of the royal family skidded to a stop in front of them, its lamps extinguished despite the darkness. Four mounted royal guards stood watch from the front and rear of the carriage. Cetrion opened the door and waved the prince inside before climbing in after him.

The driver cracked his whip and the carriage sped off through the rear gate of the palace. The guards stationed there glanced at the symbol on its side as it barreled past, but they said nothing.

The carriage's wheels rattled as it made its way down the first district's cobblestone streets, lined with the manors of various nobles.

Suddenly, the horses let out a loud whinny, and the carriage came clattering to a stop, throwing Prince Dakares forward.

"Who goes there?!"

A royal guard called out, but instead of a response, the next sound the prince heard was the clash of swords.

"Cetrion, what's going on out there?"

Prince Dakares peered out his window into the darkness, but he couldn't make out anything other than a vague movement in the inky shadows.

"Please, stay calm, Your Highness. There is nothing to fear."

Cetrion reached down, drew the intricately decorated saber from his waist, and thrust it straight into the prince's heart.

The prince looked confused, staring down at the silver blade sticking out of his chest. His eyes found Cetrion's.

"But...but why?"

Blood frothed at the corners of his mouth, and his head fell back.

The door to the carriage opened, and a man climbed in.

Cetrion nonchalantly pulled the saber from the prince's chest, wiped it clean, and returned it to its sheath before dropping to one knee.

"It seems all went according to plan. Well done."

A tall, handsome man with light brown hair smiled down at Cetrion. "I am not worthy of such praise."

Cetrion looked up at the man in front of him—Sekt Rondahl Karlon Rhoden Sahdiay, the first prince of the Rhoden Kingdom.

"Still, I'm quite impressed that you were able to put this together so quickly."

"I already knew that multiple beastmen were lurking near the palace. I told the officials at the Etzat Market to come to me at the first sign of trouble."

"How clever. And how fortuitous that the seeds of dissent we planted back in Houvan would produce such fruit here." Prince Sekt's handsome face twisted into a disturbed grin.

"Yes, that plan was used to great effect with Princess Yuriarna. I've already disposed of the person I made arrangements with."

"I've known what Yuriarna was up to for some time now. However, between the monsters and losing half of our forces, I assumed the Houvan revolt would be delayed."

"Considering those monsters created our current situation, I'd say we got lucky."

"True. They also rid us of that annoying priest and his followers. Anyway, I just received Yuriarna's heirloom necklace. Once everything else is settled, we can make it look like Dakares plotted her death."

Sekt frowned. "All that's left is Maldoira, then. I'm so sorry to have to ask this of you."

Cetrion shook his head. "No, it would be foolish to leave the country to a man like my father. He's committed to the hegemony in the east. I will honor my forefathers by resolving this before it gets any worse."

"And the rest will go as planned?"

"Correct."

The two exchanged a look, and with a nod from Prince Sekt, Cetrion once again drew his saber.

"Try not to go too deep, all right?"

Cetrion readied his blade. An instant later, he thrust it into the prince's left arm.

"Nnngaaah!"

Sekt let out a howl, his face contorting in pain. Blood gushed from the wound, staining his shirt, making the injury look far more severe than it actually was.

Cetrion returned his saber to its sheath and offered it to the prince.

"Please proceed as planned and get treated, Your Highness. After that, you can report on what happened here."

Prince Sekt took the sword and nodded, his brow soaked with sweat.

Cetrion hopped out of the carriage and ordered the driver to hurry to the temple. He stepped back as the crack of a whip broke the silence of the empty streets. A moment later, the lamps on the carriage flickered on as it took off at full speed, its wheels rattling along the cobblestones.

After seeing the carriage off, Cetrion turned to several knights standing nearby and pointed to a location off in the distance.

"Make your way to the Etzat Market, and hurry."

The tone in the lieutenant general's quiet voice sent a chill down the knights' spines.

The Etzat Market—the largest slave-trading center in the entire capital—was located in Olav's third district. It had been built near the wall leading to the second district, and it always boasted a large number of patrons.

The market traded in numerous types of slaves, including humans. The reasons for enslavement varied, but often included criminals, children put up as collateral for a debt, and people taken as war prizes.

In addition to humans, there were also the so-called beastmen—non-humans who'd been ripped from their homes and sold as if they were property. The market handled all of these sales.

These beastmen, who referred to themselves as the mountain people, were marked by their animal-like ears and tails and were feared for their superior physical abilities, which was why they'd been driven out from wherever humans lived. However, that same physical prowess made them highly desirable on the slave market. They could be put to use in coal mines and other harsh working conditions where humans didn't want to venture.

The majority of beastmen captured in the central part of the Rhoden Kingdom ultimately ended up as slaves in the capital, where they were used for manual labor by nobles and the wealthy, leading to a massive concentration of slave houses in Olav.

The Etzat Market was the biggest of these, both in terms of the number of slaves sold and the sheer size of its massive building.

The imposing, four-story monstrosity was surrounded by high walls on all sides and sported a massive gate reinforced with iron rivets. It was nothing like the buildings surrounding it.

Down a nearby side street, several people peered out of the shadows at the sturdy-looking gate.

Ariane wore her charcoal cloak low over her head as she usually did, to cover her amethyst skin and pointy ears. Next to her, a large man dressed all in black crouched low, trying to conceal his massive frame.

I had seen this man before.

He was the man at the center of the scuffle Ariane and I had witnessed when we first came to the capital. He'd traded his turban for the same black, metal-reinforced headgear that Chiyome wore, which covered his head and mouth.

His upper body, however, was bare, revealing his bronze, muscular skin. He wore simple metal gauntlets on each arm.

I was hardly one to comment on appearance, considering how I looked, but he certainly struck an interesting figure.

Chiyome had brought him to assist us in attacking the Etzat Market. He was a beastman just like Chiyome, and his name was Goemon, another of the six elite members of the Jinshin clan.

Unlike Chiyome, however, his hair was silver and black, almost like a tabby cat's. With his dark skin and massive frame, he reminded me more of a tiger than a house cat. I couldn't help but wonder if there was a fandom out there that would be interested in this brawny, cat-eared mountain of a man.

Between the darkness of the night and the lack of lamps, my vision was limited. However, I could just make out a vague, shadowy figure moving along the tops of the walls that surrounded the Etzat Market. The shadow effortlessly leaped to the ground and silently approached the alley where we were hiding.

It was Chiyome. She wore a crimson scarf wrapped around her neck, which waved about like a tail as she moved. She skidded to a stop in front of us and gave a report on the status of the other squads preparing to attack the market.

"The others are in place, so all we need to do is draw out as many guards as we can."

She'd changed out of her earlier disguise and was now wearing ninja attire, allowing her to melt into the darkness. Even just watching the way she ran, I was convinced she truly was a ninja. And her night vision and nimble movements accentuated her cat-like qualities.

Chiyome gave me a satisfied grin, almost as if she could read my mind. "We are the mountain people, chosen by our great founder, Hanzo. And the cat people are the most gifted of all."

My brain translated this as, *"Furries are awesome! All praise the cat ears!"*

Still, something about what she'd said caught my attention. "Was your great founder also a cat person?"

"No, Hanzo was a human. He'd been working as a spy for the Revlon Empire and started taking cat people under his wing to save them from their poor treatment. That was the start of the Jinshin clan."

"Oh? So, you're no longer associated with the empire?"

"That's right. We were originally a spy organization under the control of the founder, but the more successful we became, the more they began to fear his power. Eventually, they began trying to assassinate him, but he dodged every attempt."

Chiyome frowned.

Nobles always feared those who took power for themselves. What's more, I imagined it didn't help Hanzo's reputation that he'd surrounded himself with cat people rather than humans.

"Soon after that, there was a battle over succession to the throne. The great founder worked behind the scenes to keep both sides fighting. He led the clan away from the empire amid the turmoil of a massive civil war."

I wondered if this Hanzo had ultimately caused the empire to be split in two.

"Hey, shouldn't we be getting started?" Ariane spoke up.

Goemon, who'd been silent this whole time, nodded.

Chiyome spoke to me. "All right, just like we planned, I'll leave the main gate up to Goemon and Arc. Is that all right with you?"

I nodded. "Not a problem. Goemon and I will take care of anyone at the gate."

Goemon shot me a grim smile.

Chiyome turned to Ariane. "We'll head to the back of the market and enter through there. Follow me." As soon as the words left her mouth, she was bounding down the road, running along the wall like a shadow. Ariane easily followed the young girl's lead.

I turned toward Goemon. He seemed to read my thoughts and moved his hulking frame out of the alley and into the street. I followed him until we were both standing in front of the main gate.

"Let's do this!"

On my mark, we began running toward the massive double doors, Goemon easily keeping pace with me. I could hear him chanting in a low voice as he braced himself.

"Muscle to stone, wall smasher!"

Light enveloped his body. A moment later, stone armor appeared across his massive shoulders.

Apparently, he could also use ninjutsu. Or maybe that was just normal magic here?

"Nnnngaaaaaaaaaaaaw!"

"Hwaaaaaaaaaaaaaaa!"

Our shouts echoed through the night, reverberating down the surrounding streets as the stone-encased Goemon and I ran headlong into the double doors. The iron-reinforced wood splintered under the impact of our bodies, showering the courtyard inside the walls.

Guards looked up in disbelief at the two intruders who'd just smashed their way in.

One of them tried to whisper to his comrade, his voice comically loud. "Is that a...ghost?"

I had tied a rope around my waist to keep my armor fully concealed under my cloak, making me look like a black phantom. I also wore the eerie festival mask that I'd bought earlier today, its hollow sneer and feathered adornments giving me an altogether unsettling appearance. "Ominous" was the word Ariane had used.

I probably did look like a ghost. I kind of liked it.

Several of the guards continued to stand there, frozen in fear. Goemon moved quickly—more quickly than someone of his size should have been able to—and sent them flying with a single punch.

"Invaders! We're under attack!"

"It's a beastman! Someone call for support!"

The remaining men came to their senses and started yelling. A few guards near the entrance raised their weapons and began advancing on us.

Right about now, Chiyome and Ariane should have been entering the building through the rear.

One of the dozen or so men surrounding us sneered at Goemon. "What's a beast doing showing its face around a human city?! Are you trying to disrupt the operations of the Etzat Market?!"

The men tightened their circle, blocking our exit. Another one, a particularly sinister-looking man, edged even closer, smirking.

"You've really got it coming to ya now, you sons of—"

Without thinking, I punched him in the face, knocking him backward. The atmosphere immediately grew much tenser, the men hungry for blood.

A rugged man, possibly their leader, shouted above the others. "We're gonna teach 'em a lesson they'll never forget...even if it kills us!"

The men cried out in unison. One of them, dressed more like a mercenary than a guard, swung his blade at me. Glenys would have been incredibly disappointed with his technique. I easily dodged the blow and swung my arm into the man's face. I heard a dull crunch as the man tumbled back into the wall, his nose and teeth shattered.

Another man lunged in. I caught his blade on my gauntlet and punched him in the ribs. He dropped to his knees, gasping for air.

Considering the caliber of men I'd be dealing with, I'd figured my sword and shield would be overkill, so I'd left them on my bed back at the inn. Even in only my armor, I was a weapon in my own right.

Two men in light armor thrust their spears at me in unison. I evaded their attacks and grabbed the spears, snapping the shafts. Then I delivered a punch to each of them.

"Gwaugh!"

"Urgh!"

The two men collapsed, eyes wide, their armor bearing fist-shaped indentations.

Goemon was also facing off against several men at once. Unlike me, however, he was much more skilled, and easily dispatched his foes. Despite his large frame, he was able to deftly dodge attacks with very little movement, allowing him to immediately counterattack with his massive fists. I watched with amazement as he took out opponent after opponent.

While my attention was on Goemon, I felt something strike my shoulder armor with an awful metal-on-metal scraping sound.

A brash voice spoke up from behind me.

"Hee hee! Forgot to watch yer back, huh?"

I turned. A man had thrust his sword right into my shoulder. However, all he'd managed to do was slice my cloak. The armor underneath had stopped the blade from going any farther.

I grabbed the tip of the sword between my fingers.

The man tried to yank it away, but he was no match for my strength. He retreated, drawing a short sword from a sheath strapped to his lower back.

"You fool!"

I gripped the stolen sword with both hands—one on the hilt, the other on the tip—and started to *bend*. The sword snapped in half with an ear-splitting clang. I tossed both pieces unceremoniously at the man's feet.

"Wh-wha?!"

While he stood there, stunned, I threw a face-deforming punch, sending him into several other men who'd been standing behind him. They all sprawled on the ground, unmoving.

In the span of only a few minutes, we'd cleared the entire courtyard in front of the gate. Goemon and I were the only ones left standing, surrounded by the sounds of groaning men.

More guards appeared, gathering around the gate, probably drawn by the commotion we'd caused.

A man who looked like he was in charge pointed his spear toward me and demanded our surrender in a commanding tone. "Just who in the hell do you think you are?! Stop what you're doing and get on the ground at once!"

"More playthings?" I murmured to myself as I turned to face him.

"Wh-what is that thing?"

"Is that a beastman?!"

Even the commander who'd demanded our surrender was stunned into silence. I laughed, and the commander's face turned a bright shade of red.

"Subdue the invaders!!!"

A dozen or so men with spears at the ready moved in to surround us, just as the mercenaries had done before. However, unlike the mercenaries, who'd attacked us one by one, we were now dealing with well-trained soldiers. They came at us in pairs, or in groups as large as six to eight men at once.

In an effort to keep them back, Goemon grabbed one of the fallen mercenaries and hurled the man's body toward the soldiers.

The body crashed into the soldiers and knocked them to the ground. Now that their line was broken, Goemon moved in to attack, though he was immediately met with spears from the remaining guards. He easily jumped over their feeble thrusts, launching a series of kicks that threw the men back like scarecrows caught in the wind.

The few guards still standing saw their chance and lunged with their spears the moment he landed.

"Muscle to metal, arm bracer! Graaw!" Goemon's deep voice echoed above the din as he assumed a pose reminiscent of a bodybuilder. His flexed muscles glimmered slightly, taking on the metallic finish of real bronze. The spears bent as they hit his body, unable to penetrate his skin.

"What's his body made of?!"

Goemon took advantage of the soldiers' confusion and delivered a series of blows that elicited screams of pain and terror.

He was almost finished with his group, apparently.

I turned my attention to the men advancing on me, only to find that every single one of them wore a look of apprehension.

To avoid being struck from behind again, I kept my body constantly moving, my arms outspread as I waited for one of them to make the first move. From their point of view, it probably looked like this man in the ominous mask was performing some sort of eerie dance. None of them moved.

"If you're just going to stand there, I guess I'll come to you instead!"

I rushed forward.

"Waugh! He's coming!"

The guards formed ranks and thrust out their spears. However, the thin wooden shafts snapped easily against my Belenus Holy Armor.

"Gwaaaaugh!"

I crashed through the line of men, sending them tumbling about like bowling pins. Those left standing threw down their spears and reached for their swords, but I delivered a flurry of punches before any of them could draw.

"Damn! Fall back, fall back!!!"

Someone issued the order to retreat, and the soldiers scattered. I started to pursue them until I noticed several arrows flying past me from behind.

I batted the arrows away and turned my attention to the new group of guards now standing at the gate. This time, they'd mustered an even larger force. Their commander issued an order, and all of the archers drew their bows in unison.

"Goemon!"

"Hmm?"

My warning reached him just as the soldiers launched their second volley.

Goemon and I retreated, evading the volley, our backs nearly up against the building. Shield-bearers stepped in front of the archers, followed by a line of spear-wielding soldiers like before. They advanced slowly.

It looked like they planned to use an entire regiment to crush just the two of us.

I glanced at Goemon. He shot me another smile.

I gave him a thumbs-up. He might not have understood exactly what it meant, but I think the meaning got across.

It was time to end this.

No matter how large this trading office might be, at the end of the day, they could only pack so many soldiers into the courtyard. Being crammed into a confined space, where their numbers counted less, was one of the greatest dangers a military force could face.

"Muscle to stone, rock spear strike!"

Goemon crossed his arms over his chest before punching them both straight into the ground. Spear-shaped rocks thrust up from the ground, one after another, slowly encircling us.

"Rock Fang!!!"

This was a mid-level area-of-effect spell from the Magus class. It caused numerous fang-shaped stones to rip up out of the earth, almost as if a giant beast was chewing its way out of the ground to swallow the soldiers whole.

"It's a mage!"

"Fall back! We'll die if we stay here!"

The line of soldiers halted their forward march and threw down their weapons, bolting for the gate. Goemon's ninjutsu and my magic pursued them for a ways until the two attacks crashed into each other with a thunderclap that caused the very earth to shake beneath us.

But somehow, instead of dissipating, the attacks combined. A large rock covered in thorns exploded from the center of the courtyard, sending stone splinters raining down on the buildings and surrounding streets in every direction.

Goemon and I sought refuge in the entrance to the building, glancing back and forth from the plumes of dirt and screaming men to each other.

Goemon's eyes were wide with surprise. "That was... unexpected."

I could only nod in response. Rather than cancel each other out, when the ninjutsu and magic had collided, they'd become far more aggressive. I wondered if a similar thing happened when mages fought each other. But judging by Goemon's reaction, he'd never seen anything like this before.

Too focused on the strange event that had just unfolded, Goemon and I failed to register the disconcerting creak coming from the building behind us.

"Huh?!"

By the time we looked up, a portion of the roof was falling toward us.

Chiyome and Ariane were atop the wall, checking out the area behind the Etzat Market as planned, when they heard a thunderous roar erupt from the entrance.

"Sounds like it's already started."

"Seems so."

"Kyii!" Ponta seemed to be voicing its agreement from where it clung to Ariane's shoulder.

A narrow, unlit path ran along the back perimeter of the trading office, bathed in blackness. Even the dim light of the moon couldn't seem to reach the area. However, Chiyome's and Ariane's species both had excellent night vision.

Chiyome looked down, eyes narrowed. "Looks like there aren't any guards back here."

"That's good for us, at least. Let's head in."

Ariane hopped from the wall and used her magic to summon a series of rocks from the ground, forming steps. She descended to the ground, her charcoal cloak waving in the wind, then ducked behind the building, becoming one with the shadows...except for Ponta, who stuck out like a sore thumb.

Chiyome jumped down behind her, landing in a crouch. Her eyes scanned the perimeter.

The windows in the back of the stone building were located well above the ground, leaving them with no obvious means of entry. She darted over to one corner, peeking her head around for a look.

"Ariane, I found an entrance on the side of the building. We'll enter through there."

The young ninja girl dashed off toward a wooden door reinforced with a sheet of metal. Ariane arrived a moment later, sighing as she spied a metal lock on the door.

"Want me to blow it open with magic?"

Chiyome shook her head. She then reached into her pocket and pulled out a thin metal pick, which she inserted in the keyhole. After a few seconds, Ariane heard a loud click followed by the sound of a bolt moving. Chiyome removed the now-open lock.

"That's amazing, Chiyome!"

The ninja girl's cheeks flushed at Ariane's praise. The door creaked as she pushed it open and slipped inside.

The interior of the building was lit by only a few dim magic lamps, making it hard to see. This had the benefit of making some areas all the darker, allowing Chiyome to blend into the shadows with ease.

"There are two attackers at the entrance!"

"Remember what we were told! Send a runner to the palace!"

The two women could hear men shouting, the urgency clear in their voices.

Ariane was about to slip through the door after Chiyome when an armed mercenary came running toward her.

"Wh-who the hell are you?!"

Before the man could raise the alarm, Chiyome dove from the shadows and stabbed him through the throat with a dagger, preventing him from making any further noise—not even a dying scream. The man clawed at his throat as he collapsed. Chiyome tried to drag him into the shadows where he wouldn't be seen, but after watching her struggle to move the dead weight for a solid minute, Ariane traded places with the cat girl. She stuffed the dead man into a dark corner.

"Thank you, Ariane."

"Leave the brute strength stuff to me. Now, let's get on with this while those two are still providing a distraction out front."

The two of them moved deeper into the building, stepping out of the narrow corridor and into a room with a vaulted ceiling, its walls lined with iron-barred cages. People of all different shapes, sizes, and species were shoved inside.

Some were cat people similar to Chiyome. Others ranged from people with the ears and tails of wolves to those with long rabbit ears. They were all keenly watching and listening.

Unlike the elves, the mountain people had little in the way of magical affinity, so none of them were wearing any sort of magical restraints like the mana-eater collar. What they lacked in magical abilities, however, they made up for in physical strength. In order to restrict their movements, they'd each had their ankles cuffed together.

Ariane took a quick look around. "It looks like every single one of these cells is for the mountain people."

Some of the people had started to take notice of Chiyome and Ariane, their eyes going wide.

"What are you...?" A voice called out from one of the cells, drawing the attention of a group of watchmen, who started yelling as they charged toward Chiyome.

"Who the hell are you? Where'd you come from?!"

"I've got him, Chiyome!" Ariane drew her sword, rushing toward the watchmen.

Her opponents already had their weapons out and were prepared to fight, but there was only enough room for two of them to stand side by side in the narrow hallway. Ariane slashed her blade as she deftly slipped between the first two men, landing on the other side.

The watchmen turned in surprise, only to slump to the floor, their blood pooling on the stones. Ariane pointed her blade toward the next two, her golden eyes narrowing within her charcoal cloak.

Faced with her impressive swordsmanship and imposing demeanor, the rest of the watchmen chose to turn and flee rather than engage her in combat.

Ariane frowned. The watchmen weren't the only ones afraid. The mountain people in the cells were cowering at the sight of her.

Chiyome lowered her black mask. "My name is Chiyome, of the Jinshin clan. We have come here to save you. Please listen to what I tell you, and I will get you all out of here."

She pulled out her lockpick and inserted it into the keyhole of the nearest cell. A moment later, the metal door opened with a screech. The people in the newly opened cell murmured to each other.

"Did she say the Jinshin clan?!"

"I can't believe it! They came to save us?" The Jinshin clan was known by practically all the mountain people.

The prisoners' eyes all began to light up with rekindled hope—a hope that had been nearly extinguished in their time locked away in their cells.

Chiyome called out above the chatter. "Can anyone here smash open these locks?"

Several people raised their hands. Chiyome undid the clasps around their ankles and handed several more picks to the newly freed slaves.

"Split up and set our comrades free! I want anyone who can fight to arm themselves with the watchmen's weapons."

"Hoorah! Leave it to us!"

While Chiyome worked quickly to free more of her trapped comrades from their cells, she started giving orders to the ragtag group of slaves, who were reveling in their newfound freedom.

"Men, take the weapons. I want the women to provide support!"

The mountain people followed Chiyome's commands, freeing their fellow slaves and arming themselves.

Just then, a contingent of soldiers wearing matching armor came rushing down the stairwell behind Ariane. They drew their swords in unison as their commander issued orders.

"Don't let the slaves or intruders get away! Kill anyone you can't capture!"

A shadow darted forward.

"Body to water, liquid wolf fang!"

Chiyome drew a symbol in the air as she ran toward the soldiers, looking like a character out of a ninja comic book. The next instant, three wolves, about a meter long each, appeared around her and rushed in to attack.

The commander watched, aghast. "Just who is this, some kind of mage?!"

The ninjutsu water wolves ducked and weaved between the men's swords, biting their ankles and sending them screaming to the ground.

Whenever a soldier was lucky enough to strike one of the wolves, the sword swished through the water with no obvious effect.

Ariane was frozen in place, watching Chiyome carry out her attack. She shook her head, coming to her senses, and launched herself at the soldiers from behind. The two women continued to move through the men, dispatching soldiers left and right. A moment later, having made quick work of the remaining watchmen, the armed slaves came to Chiyome and Ariane's aid.

With the full brute strength of the mountain people arrayed against them, the soldiers could no longer hold their position. One by one, they were slaughtered and robbed of their weapons. As the number of resistance fighters increased, the number of soldiers dwindled.

Around seventy slaves had joined the fray when another thunderous roar echoed in the distance. A moment later, the entire building shook as a blast of wind and dirt blew through the hallways, extinguishing the oil lamps and blanketing the rooms in darkness.

The fighting stopped as everyone froze. But as soon as the roar had passed, the clash of swords resumed. Unlike the mountain people with their superior night vision, the humans were essentially fighting blind, unable to clearly make out who they were fighting and, in some cases, killing their fellow soldiers.

Once the majority of the soldiers and watchmen had been dealt with, the ex-slaves began checking each other's injuries. Around that time, two hulking shadows appeared from direction of the main entrance.

One of them looked to be around thirty years old. He was two meters tall and naked from the waist up. The other was covered from neck to toe in a black cloak and wore an eerie mask adorned with feathers, lending him an unsettling aura. Both were completely covered with dust.

The mountain people froze, instantly gripped with fear.

The first man was one of them, but the other...they couldn't say. Uncertain what to do about the approaching men, the mountain people looked desperately to Ariane and Chiyome.

Ponta cried out excitedly, its cotton tail wagging excitedly at the sight of the newcomers.

"Kyii! Kyiiiii!"

Ariane let out a loud sigh and threw back her hood, revealing her amethyst skin and pointed ears. The ex-slaves watched her in stunned silence, having assumed that both of their rescuers were from the Jinshin clan.

Their surprise, however, quickly turned back to fear as the man in the ominous mask approached.

"Hah! I thought we were dead for sure."

I crawled out from under the rubble of the collapsed ceiling and brushed myself off.

The unexpected magical explosion had caused part of the first floor to cave in, giving me a clear view up into the second. The courtyard in front of the building was in complete disarray, and I could see the bodies of dozens of soldiers among the mountain of rubble.

As the wind carried the dust away and a calm silence once again descended, footsteps echoed along cobbles of the streets outside. I could tell from the sound that a large number of people were approaching, likely either more reinforcements or, if we were unlucky, the Royal Army. In either case, I didn't have any time to waste. I started digging through the rubble.

"Goemon! Goemon, are you okay?!"

As I sifted through the rubble, a musclebound arm burst out of the debris, followed by a dust-covered Goemon.

"Goemon! You're safe!"

"I'm...fine, I think."

He shook the debris from his body. The ears on top of his head twitched in the direction of the gate, and he turned his gaze to the darkened street. Apparently, he'd noticed the approaching troops as well.

"It seems like reinforcements are on the way, but I can't see them ignoring their injured allies. We might have some time before they attack. We should get the freed slaves out of here while we have a chance."

Goemon nodded in agreement and hopped down from the mountain of rubble, making his way toward the entrance to the building. I followed him inside.

After passing through the main entrance hall and another set of doors, we found ourselves in a dim dungeon lined with row upon row of empty cells. We continued deeper inside until we came to a room filled with newly freed slaves.

Many of them were cat people like Chiyome and Goemon, but there was a wide variety of other species as well, including burly wolfmen and rabbit-eared folk. It was almost like a furry expo. I approached, excited.

As the group of animal people took notice of me, looks of concern started appearing on their faces. I tilted my head in confusion. From somewhere off in the distance, I heard Ponta cry out.

I spotted Ariane, her hood lowered. She looked annoyed, which only made me more confused.

"Arc, I think you can take that mask off now. You're scaring everyone."

I'd completely forgotten how I was dressed.

"Oh, right! You know, I've actually come to like how I look with it on."

Ponta hopped off of Ariane's shoulder and glided over toward me, burying its small body in the decorative feathers atop my head.

"Kyii kyiiiii!"

This was the most excited I'd seen Ponta in a while. While I tried to calm my animal friend down, Chiyome turned to Goemon.

"How are things at the front gate?"

Usually a man of few words, Goemon responded to Chiyome's question in a low voice. "A large number of re-inforcements are on their way, but Arc and I should be able to hold them off." He pointed a thumb toward me. "You should have some time before they're able to break through."

I nodded in response, almost knocking Ponta off my head in the process. I could hear it scrabbling against the mask as it clung to the feathers and scrambled its way back atop my head.

"And how are things here, Miss Ariane? Is this everyone?"

The freed slaves had relaxed slightly now that they realized I was an ally of their rescuers.

All of the locks had been removed from the cells, but there were still a number of people in shackles, though others were working quickly to remove these.

"We're almost done here. It sounds like slaves are also kept on the upper floors, so we'll need to go deeper into the building."

Ariane turned her gaze toward a large set of doors on the far side of the room.

I thought they'd entered through the rear of the building, but apparently there wasn't any entrance back there, meaning that all entry and exit points were limited to this central room.

Chiyome and Goemon exchanged glances.

"What if we leave Goemon to take care of things here?" I asked. "That way, I can go with you. Once we free everyone else and get all of the slaves out of the capital, then the mission will be complete, correct?"

Goemon nodded.

"Got it," said Ariane.

Chiyome turned to Goemon. "All right, our final escape will take place as planned. Once the reinforcements make it inside, we'll have Goemon take out the building and Arc will teleport everyone out."

The first time I'd heard this plan, I'd balked at the idea. Even if Goemon and I were able to draw a large number of soldiers to the market, as long as we left the building standing, they would be able to easily regroup and reinforce the other slave houses.

However, the guards and royal soldiers were sent here to bring order back to the Etzat Market. They were neither murderous bandits nor corrupt slave traders.

The mercenaries, on the other hand, were. They took money to fight the enemies of whoever was paying their bills. That was no different from how things were back in my world, really.

I'd originally become a mercenary without giving it much thought, but that was only because I'd figured mercenaries were something like adventurers in this world, like they were in the game. It was a decision I was starting to regret. I wanted nothing to do with the kind of people who could so callously make the mountain people their slaves.

I nodded to Chiyome.

"Well then, let's hurry along."

We left Goemon to take care of preparing the escape while I, along with Ponta, accompanied Ariane and Chiyome through the doors on the far side of the room. They opened up to a walled garden.

On the far side of the garden was another large door, guarded by several rough-looking men.

One of the men, a particularly large fellow, had his hands around the necks of two young girls, who were twisting and writhing in his grasp. The girls had animal-like ears atop their heads and were dressed in tattered clothes.

Surprise washed over the man's face as he noticed us, though he quickly composed himself and started yelling, spittle flying everywhere.

"So, you're the bastard who came here in that stupid costume! I know who you are...you're those beast rescuers, yeah?! Well, what do ya think is about to happen to these two, huh?"

"My name is Arc, though I am no rescuer. Now, could you please let those children go?"

I stuck out my chest as I demanded the children's release...and quickly realized my folly. Here I was, dressed in a mask to hide my identity, and yet I'd just given him my name. I couldn't believe my carelessness. Still, for a moment it looked as if I'd gotten through to the large man. That is, until his face broke into a fiendish grin and he gripped the girls' throats even tighter.

"Shaddap, or that'll be the end of 'em. Now, drop yer weapons and kick 'em over here!"

Next to the shouting, musclebound man, several of the other men turned their leering gazes toward Ariane.

"Heh. What do have here? A dark elf?"

Ariane narrowed her thin eyebrows. "Using the weak as a shield is standard practice for humans, I see."

Chiyome and Ariane set their weapons on the ground and kicked them over. The men seemed oblivious to their hateful glares and laughed in response. Now that we were unarmed, they seemed to decide that we were no longer a threat and lowered their own weapons.

They couldn't have been more wrong.

Several of the men approached me. When they were still about a foot or so away, the large man called out to them. "Only kill the masked man! We'll take the other two home as prizes."

The men let out howls of laughter. Right as they were about to swing their weapons, I used Dimensional Step to teleport behind the large man.

The men's weapons cut uselessly through the air.

The large man shouted, shock evident in his voice. "Wha?! He's gone!"

I grabbed the man's head in both hands and twisted, turning it nearly completely around with a loud snap. For a moment, the man's eyes were wide in fear, then his whole body went slack. The two girls fell to the floor with a thud. Something began dripping from the man's pant leg. I tossed the body over to a nearby wall where it collapsed in a heap.

The two girls clutched their throats, gasping for breath. As their breathing started to normalize, they looked up at me in fear. I brushed my hands through their soft hair. They couldn't have been more than five or six. Their expressions relaxed as they noticed Ponta's head peeking out from among the feathers adorning my mask.

"Just close your eyes. The scary stuff will all be over in a moment."

"Kyiii..."

They both nodded and buried their faces in their hands.

"Dammit! What the hell did you do?!"

All traces of confidence had vanished from the men. They could barely conceal their horror at seeing their companion dispatched so brutally. I took advantage of their momentary lapse and rushed them, closing the distance between us in an instant.

Despite my best efforts to hold back, the men's faces and chests were torn open as I pummeled them, the sounds of shattering bones and gurgling screams filling the garden. Ariane and Chiyome retrieved their weapons and joined the fray. The whole thing was over in a matter of seconds, the garden now filled with the men's deformed bodies.

I returned to the little girls and spoke to them gently, trying not to alarm them. "You can open your eyes now. The scary old men are all gone now."

Even as the words left my mouth, I knew they sounded odd. I was hardly one to talk, considering the creepy mask I was wearing.

Ariane called out from behind me. "We're done here, Arc. Let's go farther inside." She made for the door at the far end of the garden. "As soon as we take care of the others, we can teleport out of here."

Just then, Chiyome's cat ears started twitching wildly.

"I can hear people beyond this door." She pushed it open.

The room on the other side looked like a well-decorated manor, sporting all manner of knick-knacks and a large table surrounded by chairs. If I had to guess, I'd say this was where the sales negotiations took place.

While I was looking around the room, the two girls jogged past me and darted through one of the doors running along the wall. Chiyome took off after them, followed closely by Ariane and me.

Beyond that door was a short hall leading to another door. As soon as we opened it, a horrible stench washed over us, like damp, rotting grass.

The room was full of mountain people, men and women, chained together. Most of them were nude, or close to it. Many of the women appeared to be pregnant. As soon as they caught sight of me, they grew afraid, trembling.

The young girls from the garden ran up to two women, hugging the enlarged bellies that protruded from their tattered clothes, sobbing quietly in their mothers' arms.

I suppressed the urge to retch. Someone was breeding mountain people like farm animals, probably selling the children as slaves. I wasn't sure how profitable a scheme like this could actually be, but judging by the small size of the room compared to the rest of the building, it seemed like they were still just experimenting with the idea. At least, I hoped they were.

In any case, it was an awful sight to behold.

"Miss Ariane, please look around for something these people can wear."

"G-got it."

My voice broke Ariane out of her temporary paralysis and she hurried out of the room in search of clothes.

Chiyome closed her eyes and furrowed her brow. After she'd gotten her emotions in check, she turned to me and spoke in her usual monotone voice.

"I'll take care of the locks, and then we can get everyone out of here."

"Roger."

Chiyome knelt next to one of the women and pulled a small metal pick from her pocket. She fitted it into the keyhole and rattled it around until the clasp opened and the woman's ankle was free.

I followed suit, kneeling down next to a dog-eared man. I grabbed the chain connected to his ankle cuff in both hands and ripped it apart. The man's eyes went wide at my feat of strength.

A few moments later, Ariane returned to find everyone in the room free of their restraints.

"There wasn't much in the way of clothes, so they'll have to make do with these."

She showed us a stack of linens.

I couldn't tell if they were bedsheets or curtains, but they would at least give the mountain people some dignity.

With Ariane's help, we passed the linens out to everyone in the room.

"Arc, we should get these people out of the city first."

"Right. Let's bring them all to the main hall."

Chiyome led the way. The people murmured among themselves, unsure what was about to happen to them. I made my way to the center of the group and shepherded everyone together. Then I focused my mind.

"Transport Gate!"

A large pillar of light, far larger than anything I'd created thus far, rose up from the floor, illuminating the dim room.

The people tensed as the light began to envelop them, their animal ears at stiff attention.

The world blinked out for an instant. A mere second later, we found ourselves standing in a moonlit field. A gentle wind rippled through the grass in waves, carrying with it the sounds of insects. Off to the south, the outline of Olav stood stark against the sky.

I found this spot after purchasing my mask earlier. I couldn't see the capital as clearly now as I could under the afternoon sun, but it was still far brighter than any other towns I'd seen.

Once they realized where they were, the people began cheering, crying, and asking Chiyome for an explanation. Those closest to me, however, took a few steps away. Not a single person tried to ask me anything.

After a few moments, the rabbit-eared mother of one of the girls I'd saved approached me and bowed her head, her eyes filled with tears. In between sobs, she expressed her gratitude.

"Th-thank you for saving my…"

As I nodded my masked head solemnly, more and more people began making their way toward me.

Under the dim light of the moon, I could barely make out another cat person, dressed in the same ninja attire as Chiyome.

Chiyome approached the figure and waved me over. She addressed the crowd in her usual monotone. "These people here will lead you to a safe place. Please, do what they say!"

After exchanging glances among each other, the crowd began to form up and follow the cat ninja.

"We'll leave the rest to them while we head back for the others."

"All right then, let's go!"

I called up Transport Gate again and teleported us back to the main hall of the Etzat Market.

A small pillar formed at our feet. A moment later, we were back in the center of the hall...and right in the middle of a group of armed animal men.

"Wha...who's there?!"

The men let out howls of surprise at our sudden appearance, though the concern on their faces faded as soon as they recognized us as the ones who'd broken them out of their cells.

A middle-aged man with drooping dog ears stepped forward from the group. "Apologies! We didn't realize it was you. We've been looking for our comrades who were locked away in here. Have you seen them?"

Chiyome pulled the mask away from her mouth and filled them in on the situation. "We've rescued them and taken them out of the capital. My fellow clan members are bringing them somewhere safe as we speak."

The other men looked comforted to hear this, but the dog-eared man narrowed his eyes. "Are you daft?! How could you get them out in such a short time?"

Rather than respond to the question, Chiyome glared at the man. "We don't have time for an explanation right now. How are the escape preparations and defense efforts going?"

The dog-eared man's eyes remained narrowed, but he provided a simple update on the situation. "All of the people are out of their cells, and about half are unchained. Soldiers are only coming into the building sporadically, but they've solidified their lines outside."

Chiyome nodded, then turned her gaze back to me.

I used Transport Gate to teleport us to the field.

Chiyome and I left the confused beastmen to her allies and teleported back to the manor, this time heading through the large door and back into the cell-lined room.

A large group of mountain people stood outside their cells, some still busy trying to break the chains from their ankles, while others fought off an attack from incoming soldiers.

It didn't look like we had a lot of time left before the main force entered the building, so I started ferrying people to the grassy field. After several trips back and forth, all of the hundred or so slaves had been transported away from the Etzat Market.

Given how much time we'd wasted trying to explain things to the confused, surprised, and grateful people who came rushing up to us, I couldn't help but wonder if it would have been faster to simply teleport them, cells and all, to begin with.

I'd been hesitant to do that, though, since sooner or later, someone would have discovered the missing cells.

While I was thinking about how we might have done things differently, Ariane spoke up.

"All that's left is the final step of the plan."

I gave a quick nod and called up an image of the building in my mind. "I'll be right back."

In a flash, I was back in the Etzat Market, alone.

The building was now empty of all life, filled with an eerie silence.

Well, not entirely empty. One figure stood alone in the darkness, the outline of his massive, well-toned body and cat ears dark against the darker shadows. It was Goemon.

He stood dead still, almost like a statue, only moving

his eyes to look over in my direction as I teleported in. His cat ears remained focused on the door.

"We have company."

A moment later, heavy footfalls filled the air, sounding almost like an avalanche rolling in. The damaged building creaked, and dust shook loose from the ceiling. Moments later, the entire entrance was filled with soldiers carrying massive shields, and lanterns to light the way.

They'd come to crush us alive.

They must not have realized that we were able to use magic. It'd be rather trivial to wipe out their forces in such a confined space.

Actually, that wasn't entirely true. It would normally be a terrible idea to use such powerful magic indoors. The caster risked destroying the building while they were still inside.

Next to me, Goemon raised both arms straight up into the air. Then he lowered them slowly, the veins on his pectoral muscles bulging as he did. His usual blank expression changed ever so slightly as his eyes narrowed. I could tell he was grinning wildly beneath his wrappings.

"How about an encore of our previous performance, Arc?"

I was pretty sure I knew what he meant by that, but I

didn't have time to clarify. "If you're sure, Goemon. Let's make this a big one, yeah?"

Goemon's grin widened, his muscles bulging. He was pretty terrifying when he smiled, actually.

"Muscle to stone, rock spear strike!"

He clanged his gauntlets together, then smashed both of his fists into the ground. The floor beneath him tore open, and fang-shaped stone spikes began ripping down the hall toward the oncoming troops.

"Rock Fang!"

I summoned my area-of-effect spell right after Goemon unleashed his ninjutsu attack. The force of the fang-shaped stones tearing out of the floor knocked even more of the ceiling loose, the ninjutsu mingling with my magic as they both hurtled away from us. The soldiers crouched behind their massive shields for cover.

Just then, a loud bang erupted as the magic and ninjutsu came fully together, expanding in size. A large stone pillar ripped up out of the ground and straight through the ceiling, countless spikes launching out of it to tear through the walls, floor, and anything else that stood in their way.

The soldiers abandoned their defensive posture, scattering as the room began to fall apart around them. A massive crash reverberated through the small space, and the whole building shook violently.

The building groaned, as if it could no longer support its own weight. Slowly but surely, the Etzat Market began to collapse in on itself. I could sense that all of the buildings connected to it would also fall, one by one, like a line of dominos.

"Let's get out of here, Goemon!"

Goemon nodded.

I summoned up Transport Gate and teleported us out into the field overlooking the capital.

My ears were still ringing from the horrendous din we'd just escaped, the sound all the more obvious in the middle of a quiet field. I shook my head, brushing the debris off of my body.

Chiyome called out to me. "I can't thank you enough for all your help, Arc."

I turned around to find the young ninja and several others dressed in similar attire. Goemon and Ariane stood among them.

Goemon silently extended a hand. I clasped it, and we shook. Then he stepped back and flexed one massive bicep. I wasn't really sure what that meant, so I assumed the same pose and flexed mine back.

"Until next time."

And that was all I got from the taciturn man before he stepped back into the group.

I reached up to remove my mask. As soon as I pulled it off, I heard a sad *kyiii* as Ponta dropped to the ground. I bowed my head in apology. "Sorry about that, Ponta."

"Arc, you're just awful."

Ariane swooped in to pick up my furry companion, rubbing Ponta against her cheek and babbling to it. She probably didn't realize that anyone could hear her, but the sound of her voice sent a warm, fuzzy feeling through my bones.

Chiyome interrupted my thoughts. "Thank you so much, Ariane and Arc, for everything. You were an immense help."

It was the most cheerful I'd heard her sound yet.

Ariane smiled back brightly, Ponta still snuggled deep in her arms.

"Don't worry about it. We had our reasons, after all."

"That's right," I said. "We need your information. Anyway, where will you be going now?"

Chiyome looked over her shoulder and gestured toward the black outline of a mountain range.

"We're headed for a village hidden in the Calcut Mountains."

Ariane looked confused. "Don't you have a large country all to yourselves on the southern continent?"

Chiyome's face clouded over with sadness at the mere mention of it. "That's true, but it'd be difficult to take such a large group of people across the ocean. Besides, a lot of the people prefer the climate here."

The group of newly freed slaves making their way toward the Calcut Mountains had grown to over two hundred strong. I wondered if the people rescued from the other attacks had all gathered here as well.

There were probably also a fair amount of people already living at their destination. A large-scale exodus of mountain people would be quite a challenge—finding safe routes to travel all while staying out of sight and dodging mercenaries and hunters,

Chiyome looked out across the mass of people and muttered to herself, a worried look on her face. "If only we knew where the shrine was..." She shook her head and turned her attention back to Ariane and me. "Anyway, don't worry about it. Besides, I owe you two information. The person you're looking for, Drassos du Barysimon, is a viscount in the Holy East Revlon Empire."

The wind suddenly picked up, sending my cloak fluttering noisily in the wind.

It looked like our journey was going to take us beyond the borders of the Rhoden Kingdom.

Epilogue

THE GRAND DUCHY of Limbult was located to the southeast of the Rhoden Kingdom.

Though originally a part of the Rhoden Kingdom itself, after the war six hundred years ago, Duke Ticient had sought to reconcile with the elves. He and several of his allies broke away from the Rhoden Kingdom to form the Grand Duchy of Limbult.

The Rhoden Kingdom wasn't pleased with the formation of the Grand Duchy, but having just suffered a defeat at the hands of the elves, and already exhausted of resources, they could do little about the situation.

The Grand Duchy immediately went about making good on Duke Ticient's promise and worked toward reconciliation. Today, they were the only human nation to have any form of trading relationship with the elves.

The humans were enamored of the high-quality magical items created by the elves, and they were always in high demand. Even in the Rhoden Kingdom, elven items and skills were highly prized. However, as a result of the massive victory the elves had managed against their aggressors despite their inferior numbers, the Great Canada Forest had kept itself closed off to the Rhoden Kingdom—then the second largest country on the continent, right behind the Revlon Empire.

Several other countries were also interested in the elves' abilities, but after seeing the fate that befell the Rhoden Kingdom, they were left with no option but to change tactics from trying to take what they wanted by force to opening trade relations.

The elves, however, burrowed deeper into the Great Canada Forest, refusing to trade with anyone but the Grand Duchy of Limbult. This gave the Grand Duchy the exclusive right to sell the elves' magical goods to other countries, greatly increasing their wealth. In spite of its small size, the Grand Duchy's power only continued to grow.

Limbult, the capital of the Grand Duchy, was built overlooking the massive port of Aldoria to the east. Ships flying the flags of countries throughout the northern continent visited the port, lending an exciting vitality to the city.

Thanks to this, Limbult boasted a larger population than even Rhoden's capital of Olav. The city was filled with all manner of magical items obtained from the elves, which merchants from across the continent—as well as the crews that manned their ships—were constantly purchasing and reselling. The city was so busy that it could easily have been mistaken for the seat of an empire.

Limbult was also the only human city where you might actually catch a glimpse of an elf.

Amid this exciting chaos, a procession of over one hundred soldiers, some wearing unfamiliar-looking armor, marched up the roads of Limbult, leading a black, horse-drawn carriage to the palace.

The carriage carried Yuriarna Merol Melissa Rhoden Olav, the second princess of the Rhoden Kingdom. She wore her blond hair straight, with a slight curl at the tips. Her brown eyes, contrasting nicely with her snow-white skin, gazed out the window of the carriage at the bustling city of Limbult. The scenery reflected in her large eyes as it slowly passed them by.

It had been twelve days since the ambush in the forest near the Anetto Mountains.

After the ambush, the procession had sped toward Limbult, avoiding all major routes that might give their attackers a second chance. They were only slightly off schedule crossing the Librout River, which marked the border between Rhoden and Limbult.

As soon as they entered the Grand Duchy, the princess paid a visit to Marquis du Braht, who ruled the surrounding area, to explain their situation and ask for protection.

The surviving contingent of thirty guards was exhausted by the time they entered Limbult. Even if their injuries from the ambush had been miraculously healed, many of them were still without horses, and all of them had spent the rest of the trip on constant alert, watching out for a follow-up strike.

Marquis du Braht allowed Princess Yuriarna and her guards to rest at his castle while he sent a messenger off to Limbult to notify Duchess Seriarna. Three days later, the messenger returned to du Braht's castle with the duchess' reply and a contingent of soldiers to escort Princess Yuriarna from Braht to Limbult.

Her carriage was now crossing the massive stone bridge leading to the duke's royal palace at the center of Limbult. A massive moat, filled with water from the nearby ocean, surrounded the palace. A number of peasants idly fishing from the sides of the bridge watched as the impressive procession rolled past.

Once across the bridge, Yuriarna finally caught sight

of the pearl-white palace—the home of the duke who oversaw the entire Grand Duchy. It was absolutely stunning, sporting countless spires and intricately carved designs, its magnificence befitting the power and wealth wielded by the Grand Duchy.

Ferna spoke up from her seat beside the princess. "I see nothing has changed. It's just as beautiful as ever."

Yuriarna silently agreed.

The entrance to the palace came into sight—a majestic staircase, at the top of which stood a familiar figure in a blue gown flanked by guards in imposing armor.

The carriage entered the palace's vast courtyard, coming to a stop at the base of the stairs.

Yuriarna didn't even wait for the driver to open her door. She climbed out of the carriage herself, running up to meet the figure at the top of the stairs.

"Meria!"

"I'm glad to see you've arrived safely, Merol," the woman said, using Yuriarna's childhood nickname.

This woman was Seriarna Meria du Olav Ticient, Yuriarna's sister, and wife to the duke of Limbult.

Seriarna came running down to Yuriarna, pulling the younger woman in for a tight hug. Tears appeared in her eyes as she looked down at her younger sister. Her hair was the same shade of blond as Yuriarna's, tied back into a ponytail. The sisters also shared the same affectionate brown eyes.

"I'm so relieved that you're alive..."

"I'm sorry for worrying you, Meria..."

Yuriarna's eyes stung with barely restrained tears at her sister's words. Seriarna pulled her in closer.

Seriarna gently caressed her sister's hair. "When I heard you were assassinated by our stepbrother Dakares back in Rhoden, my world went dark. I thought my heart would stop right then and there."

Yuriarna's head bolted up. "What do you mean, Dakares?"

Seriarna looked confused. After a tense silence, she went on to explain to Yuriarna the recent events that had been going on in the Rhoden Kingdom. "I...I thought you knew. A short time ago, Dakares carried out a massive attack in the middle of Olav. He tried to murder Sekt in all of the confusion, though Sekt killed him instead, with only minimal injury to himself."

"Then what makes you say Dakares was behind my assassination?"

"When Dakares was killed, mother's heirloom necklace—the one you always wear—was found in his pocket. From what I heard, Dakares had ordered General Maldoira to carry out the attack on you."

Yuriarna's hand flew to her chest.

After the attack, she hadn't been able to find her necklace anywhere. Too worried about a second ambush, she had put her feelings aside and decided to worry about it later.

She was filled with both a strange sense of comfort and an intense anger over hearing that it had been stolen by her brother.

"What happened to General Maldoira?" Yuriarna struggled to stay calm as she asked about the man who'd led her assassination attempt.

"As the story goes, the general was also involved in letting out the beastmen in the capital in order to cause all the chaos. His son, Lieutenant General Cetrion, struck him down then and there. Since he helped save Sekt's life, he's going to be the next Duke Olsterio."

Yuriarna looked down, trying to hide the flurry of emotions racing through her mind.

Seriarna brushed a hand through her sister's hair and pulled her close again. She whispered in Yuriarna's ear.

"You're alive... That's enough for now."

The whirlwind running through Yuriarna's heart dissipated, replaced instead by an intense warmth. She buried her face in her beloved sister's neck as she fought back tears.

"Thank you, Meria. But I can't leave Sekt alone like this, or the Rhoden Kingdom will be assimilated by the Great West Revlon Empire. I need to tell Father that I'm safe and make sure that Sekt doesn't steal the crown."

Seriarna shook her head in response to her sister's plan.

"I beg you, stay here for a while. Sekt is a careful man. As long as he thinks he's the heir apparent, he won't be in any hurry to assume the throne. If you were to return to Rhoden now, he might very well succeed in killing you a second time. He might claim that your murder was all Dakares' plot, but we have no proof of that. And Dakares' former supporters haven't declared for anyone yet, so there's a possibility that they may try to come over to your side. Sekt would be a fool to risk that."

The worry in Seriarna's face left Yuriarna at a loss for words. But as a member of the royal family, she couldn't just run away. She told her sister as much, a look of unbending determination etched on her face in spite of her young age.

The duchess frowned at this. "In that case, at least fulfill the duty Father assigned you first. If you can pull that off, then it will surely serve as a great asset to you when you return to Rhoden."

Yuriarna nodded, then turned her head to look past the palace to the Great Canada Forest north of Limbult.

"You're right. First, I will meet with the elves and try to open a dialogue concerning the future of our countries' relationship. I will need your husband's assistance, however, if we are to have any chance at success."

Yuriarna looked back at her sister, the determination still evident in her eyes.

Duchess Seriarna smiled down at the young princess and squinted slightly, as if she were staring into a bright light.

The Holy Revlon Empire was located in the northeastern corner of the northern continent.

Habahren, the capital of the empire, was located at the center of its expansive territory. A picturesque city built in the midst of vast fields, Habahren was home to approximately eighty thousand people, the round, walled-off city radiating out from the castle at its center.

The castle, called Siguenza, had been built for defense rather than beauty, and had served as a fortress in the days of the old Revlon Empire.

Inside the emperor's office, deep within Siguenza, a man with a sharp nose and muddy, reddish-brown hair sat in a chair reserved for the ruler of the empire. Domitianus

Revlon Valtiafelbe, the young emperor of the Holy Revlon Empire, wore a fitted military uniform as he looked at the maps of his domain spread across his desk. His head was propped up on his fist as he gazed at the papers.

A knock came at the door.

"Come in."

The door opened hesitantly, and a chubby, mustached man dressed in the flashy garb of the imperial officials stepped inside. The man's paunch swayed slightly as he walked, a shifty smirk plastered to his face.

At a glance, the man looked like any other wealthy merchant, but he was in fact the lord chancellor of the Holy Revlon Empire, charged with handling the government's affairs. His name was Velmoas du Lyzehl.

The emperor shot the man an annoyed look. "What is it, Velmoas?"

The shifty smile never left Velmoas' face. "Ah, yes, Your Highness. We have just received a letter from our contact in Rhoden. It seems that, um, that the successor will almost assuredly be Prince Sekt."

"What?!" The emperor made no effort to conceal his anger at this unpleasant news, delivered by a man whose company he could hardly stand in the first place.

Velmoas, however, seemed to be used to this treatment, and carried on as if nothing had happened.

"That's correct. Apparently, Prince Dakares had plotted to do away with Princess Yuriarna and Prince Sekt, but ultimately it was Prince Dakares himself who was killed. And at Prince Sekt's own hand."

"Why the hell would that idiot Dakares try to carry out such a hare-brained scheme?! No one ever ran this past me!"

Domitianus' face contorted into a scowl as he unleashed a series of expletives about the late Prince Dakares.

"After the assassination of Marquis du Diento, perhaps his supporters' confidence was shaken and he was desperate to get it back?"

The Lord Chancellor's paunch jiggled slightly as he let out a crude laugh. "That's where the elves were coming from, no? Hmm...so if Sekt is the successor, then that means their relations with the heathens in the west will strengthen and we will have an even harder time expanding south."

Domitianus crossed his arms, glaring down at the maps in front of him.

Velmoas stroked his mustache. "The Monster Corps isn't quite ready for deployment, but what do you think about sending them up north to Wetrias as a trial run?"

Domitianus considered this suggestion. "Hmm, you're right. If monsters start racking up victims in Wetrias, they'll have no choice but to move their armies along the southern border. But don't send anything other than monsters. We don't want them to realize we're behind this."

Velmoas bowed ever so slightly in acknowledgement.

"After Wetrias, I was thinking we could try scattering the 'cultivation rune stones' as a trial."

"Understood. I will contact the Runeology Cloister." Velmoas hefted his stomach and leaned in even closer, as if the two were bosom companions.

Domitianus raised his head. "Speaking of, whatever happened with Fumba?"

"Ah, yes. They have been sent to the Leibnizche region, near the Karyu Mountains. There are some particularly strong monsters active out there. According to the report I received the other day, they have already caught a five-headed hydra."

Domitianus' eyes went wide. "That's...amazing. A five-headed hydra? We could easily overrun an entire town with one of those."

The hydra was a large monster that looked like a snake with four legs. They were usually found in swamps and wetlands. The longer a hydra lived, the more heads it would grow, increasing its power by leaps and bounds with each new one. Add to that its regenerative abilities and water magic, and a hydra was a force to be reckoned with.

"Fumba has it under control for now, but they're unable to get the employ ring onto its body due to its size. They'll need enough rings to put one on each of its necks in order to truly get it under their control."

"I see... In that case, have the Runeology Cloister prepare some special employ rings, and tell them to increase production of the normal ones. No matter how we plan on using the Monster Corps, we'll need to have Fumba redouble their efforts."

The corners of Emperor Domitianus' lips curled up into a wide grin.

Lahki's Merchant Diary, Part 2

A GENTLE WIND BLEW across the empty fields under the darkening, burgundy sky, an almost lonely sound carried along with it. The Hibbot wasteland stretched off to the west as far as the eye could see, growing increasingly red as the sun set. To the east, the forests running along the base of the Calcut mountain range were already submerged in purple nightfall.

A lone horse tugged a cart down the desolate, neglected road that cut through the empty plains.

A young man with messy, light brown hair steered the cart, all the while humming cheerfully to himself.

The man was in his early- to mid-twenties and clearly took care of his appearance, though he hardly looked well-to-do. Judging by the contents crammed into his cart, anyone passing by would instantly know that he was a merchant.

A young muscular man, around the same age as the driver, walked beside the cart.

From the leather armor he wore to the simple sword at his waist and small buckler on his back, it was apparent that this young man was a mercenary. He ran a hand through his short-cropped blond hair as he surveyed their surroundings.

"Hey Lahki, the sun's about to set. Think we'll hit Ura anytime soon?"

The man sitting in the driver's seat, Lahki, looked around. "Yeah, it should be pretty close. Do you want to climb aboard, Behl?"

"The cart's already piled with goods...plus that dead weight in the back. I'd feel bad for making the poor horse take on any more." The young mercenary, Behl, jogged past the horse, shouting his reply back over his shoulder with a laugh.

A woman lying in the back of the cart, her arms gently waving about as she stared off into nothingness, stirred at Behl's comment. "Waitaminnit, Behl. You're not suggesting that I'm dead weight, are you?"

The young woman was dressed in boyish clothes and wore her semi-long chestnut-colored hair tied back in a ponytail. She leaned over the side of the cart and glared at Behl.

"Hey, I never said anything about you, Rea. Why, do *you* think you're dead weight?"

Rea responded to his teasing with a shrill yell. "What was that?!"

"All right, all right. Calm down, you two. I can see the village now." Lahki admonished them in a well-practiced one.

Behl and Rea turned their attention ahead to the faint outline of the town up ahead.

Behl let out a sigh. "Finally. Why do things look so different on the east and west sides of the Calcut Mountains?"

Rea nodded in agreement and held up her waterskin, giving it a shake to check its contents.

"I know. I left with a full waterskin this morning, and it's already empty. Let's hurry into town before the sun sets."

There were two routes—east or west around the Calcut mountain range—available to those wishing to travel from Luvierte to the capital.

The east route traveled along the Lydel River and the vast, fertile fields that bordered it. Due to this, there were many villages and towns along the way, and a constant stream of traffic.

Lahki and his crew, however, had taken the western route due to its more direct path and thus shorter travel time. However, since the fields on this side were unsuitable for farming, there were few settlements. The distances between one village and the next were vast, and they rarely encountered anyone else along the way, despite this being an official road maintained by the kingdom.

There was also little in the way of animal life as a result of the harsh living conditions, though anyone who took this to mean that there were also few monsters would be sorely mistaken. In addition to the creatures that occasionally came out of the forests near the base of the Calcut Mountains, there were also incredibly powerful monsters living in the Hibbot wasteland that would sometimes roam all the way to the road. The western route was the more dangerous of the two, and required constant vigilance.

Its saving grace, at least, was that you were highly unlikely to encounter any bandits here, which was a major issue along the eastern side.

Once they got a little closer to the village, fields of beans, millet, and other hardy crops suitable for dry weather came into view. The village was surrounded by an empty moat and a wall made of sandbags, put in place by its inhabitants in a desperate attempt to protect what was theirs.

Lahki took a small path off the main road and through the fields to get to the village entrance. Villagers nearby watched with wonder as the party approached, whispering among themselves. They seemed eager to discover what was in the cart, since a merchant's arrival was a rare occurrence.

Lahki drove straight up to the village chief's house.

"We should introduce ourselves first."

Being a town of fewer than three hundred residents, Ura had no inns to speak of. It was customary in situations like this to introduce yourself to the village chief and ask for an empty house to stay in, or even for the chief to take you in.

Lahki had traveled the western route on numerous occasions and was already familiar with the chief of Ura. He took the cart into the village center and parked it in front of the only two-story house. He knocked lightly on the door, and a gaunt older woman answered it.

"Oh, Banda, it's been some time. Is the chief home?" Lahki bowed his head low.

The older woman, Banda, seemed surprised at Lahki's sudden appearance, but she smiled back at him.

"Oh my, it's been a while, Lahki m'boy. I didn't expect to see you here at a time like this."

"Hello, Ms. Banda!"

"Hi, ma'am!"

Behl and Rea leaned out from behind Lahki and greeted the woman as well. Her eyes crinkled in a warm grin.

"Oh, Behl and Rea. I see you're as chipper as ever."

Banda had come to live here many years ago when she'd married Bent, the longtime village chief of Ura. Behl and Rea had also stopped in this village many times while performing their duties as Lahki's bodyguards.

The four had just started to make small talk when a voice from inside the house chimed in.

"Quit wagging your jaw in the doorway and invite them in! Lahki, go ahead and park the cart in the usual place."

An old man with thin white hair and a dark tan stuck his head out to address Lahki. The man had a strong, masculine face and a muscular body to match. He was none other than Bent, chief of the village of Ura. After all these years living in such a harsh environment, he lacked any of the usual frailty that men in their fifties usually displayed.

Lahki and Behl took the cart around to the shed next to the house, brought the horse over to the village stable, and returned to find Rea, Banda, and Bent talking. The five of them made their way upstairs and entered the living room, which also served as the dining room and kitchen. A guest room was also located on the second floor.

The group sat around the table and sipped from wooden cups filled with water.

Bent's face hardened as he immediately launched into a question. "Lahki m'boy, you'll be traveling on through Branbayna on your way down south, I suppose?"

Lahki responded cautiously. "Yes, like usual..."

Branbayna was the largest town along the western route, and Lahki always made it a habit to stop there either before or after visiting Ura. Lahki wasn't alone in this. Nearly all travelers along the western route made their way there.

Bent and Banda exchanged a glance through narrowed eyes.

Lahki followed up with a question of his own. "Why do you ask? Did something happen in Branbayna?"

Bent shook his head and sighed. His voice took on a serious tone. "No, it's just that goblins have been showing up along the route between here in Branbayna lately..."

His three guests looked perplexed. Behl was the first to voice what they were all thinking. "Goblins? They're no big deal. A group of all the men around town should be able to take care of them."

Goblins weren't all that strong to begin with. Even in a town like Ura that didn't have much in the way of weapons, they should be able to take care of such a nuisance with no more than their farming tools.

"There are about a hundred of them. Far too many for us..."

"A hundred?!" Rea blurted out her surprise.

Even at their largest, goblin mobs usually topped out around thirty or forty. It was almost unheard of to hear of anything larger. As mercenaries, Rea and Behl had ample experience dealing with goblins and other monsters.

Lahki thought for a moment. "I wonder if they were chased off by something. Are there any other monsters around?"

"No, just goblins. No one has witnessed anything else."

Behl crossed his arms and looked up at the ceiling. "But if they *did* get chased off, maybe they won't be able to go back to wherever they came from for a while..."

Bent let out a heavy sigh. "Usually we'd hire some mercenaries in Branbayna to take care of the goblins, but there are so many along the route that we can't even get there."

Rea huffed and took a sip of her water. "Not many people use this route, so it can take a while for problems to be addressed."

Bent's face grew even more serious. "That brings us to the meat of the matter. Could I ask Behl and Rea to clear out the goblins for us? We're more than happy to pay your fees, though I know this will affect Lahki's schedule..."

Behl and Rea glanced over at Lahki. As their employer, he had the final say.

Lahki's shoulders slumped. "Well, we'd have to do something about the goblins on our way to Branbayna anyway."

Bent broke out into a smile. "Thank you, Lahki m'boy!"

Surprisingly, it was Behl's voice that butted in to rain on their parade. "That's assuming we can kill all the goblins. Twenty would be difficult enough, but a hundred? I'm not sure my blade could even hold its edge for that many."

He looked down at the sword Lahki had given him and frowned. Of course, Behl wouldn't be fighting alone, but even splitting the task with Rea, that still left them with fifty each—no easy feat. Hacking through that many goblins would do a number on his sword, and without a town nearby to sharpen it for him, that would mean continuing on to Branbayna with a dull blade—a dangerous prospect.

Lahki flashed his usual easy smile at Behl.

"Don't worry, I have an idea." He turned his attention back to the village chief. "Actually, there's something I'd like to sell you, Bent..."

The next day, around noon, a group of around a dozen men were hiding behind rocks a little ways outside the village, just off the main road, where the barren fields sloped into a gentle hill. A shallow chasm ran through the side of the hill, only about four meters deep, a simply built ladder placed inside to get to the top. The bottom of the chasm was covered with dried branches and leaves.

Each of the men huddled along the hill had a ceramic pot in front of them and a rock or other similarly hard object in their hand. Bent and Rea huddled with them. Sweat poured from the crouching villagers, trapped between the baking sun and the parched earth beneath them.

Rea craned her neck to see how things were going. A moment later, she spotted the outline of the person she was looking for.

"He's here."

With that one, simple statement, the villagers tensed in anticipation.

Lahki's heavy footfalls echoed across the landscape as he ran toward the entrance to the chasm. He didn't usually exert himself like this, his gait incredibly awkward as he ran. An ominous, unnatural cloud of dust followed closely behind as he made his mad dash toward the villagers. However, it wasn't Lahki kicking up all that dust, but a large group of green creatures.

The creatures were only about a meter tall, with thin limbs and large distended bellies. Their mouths gaped, the corners reaching almost all the way to their large, pointed ears. Smack in the middle of their faces bulged a pair of massive eyes, constantly darting around. They were each armed with a simple wooden club.

This was pretty much the same type of goblin you'd encounter anywhere throughout the continent, though they usually kept to groups of a few dozen at most—nowhere near the hundred or so here. They let out hideous, ear-piercing cries as they chased after Lahki, swinging their clubs.

Lahki hopped over a small stone wall in front of the chasm and ran straight inside, chest heaving. Moments later, the goblin mob came diving over the wall as well. Rea stood up at the top of the hill and called out.

"Lahki, hurry!"

Lahki reached the end of the chasm and started climbing the ladder. Once at the top of the hill, he collapsed, his breathing ragged. Two nearby villagers quickly grabbed the ladder and pulled it up out of the chasm. With nowhere else to go, the goblins let out another ear-piercing screech and shook their clubs at Lahki and Rea.

"Now!" Rea shouted.

In unison, Bent and all of the other villagers grabbed their pots and threw them down at the goblins. The pots shattered the moment they made contact, covering the goblins in liquid. This further incensed the goblins, who shrieked all the louder.

Unaffected, Rea waved her right hand and began to chant.

"I call upon the flames to rain down upon our foes... Fire Beretta!"

Two fist-sized balls of fire formed in the air in front of her outstretched hand, then flew off at top speed into the chasm.

One ball hit a liquid-covered goblin near the entrance and the other struck the dead leaves lining the floor. An instant later, the goblin who was hit lit up like a match and dropped to the ground, rolling around in a vain attempt to put itself out. However, this only served to set the dead grass and leaves ablaze, bathing the goblins' feet in a sea of flames. The goblins themselves began to catch fire, the chasm filling with bloodcurdling screams.

"Now's your chance! Throw the rocks!"

Lahki, somewhat recovered, held up a large stone about the size of a person's head and dropped it into the chasm below. The stone instantly felled a burning goblin. The other villagers picked up their own stones and hurled them down into the chasm while Rea continued to shoot fireball after magical fireball.

Several goblins near the entrance tried to escape the flames, but ended up crushed against the stone wall as the mob behind them surged forward. Any goblin lucky enough to make it over the wall met a quick end at the hands of Behl, who was standing by with his blade.

About ten minutes later, the goblin mob had been reduced to a pile of burning meat.

Lahki sat with a heavy thud and wiped the sweat from his brow. "Well, I'd say that went pretty well."

"Lahki m'boy, thank you so much for your help. The head of Branbayna will certainly pay you handsomely for your services. Just tell me what we owe you." Bent smiled brightly and offered Lahki his hand.

Lahki returned the smile as he calculated the total bill for their services. "Well, I'll need the money for the oil we soaked the dried grass with, Behl and Rea's fees, and the surcharge for using me as a decoy. Does four sok sound about right?"

The two shook on the deal before the party made their way back to Ura to spend the night. Early the next morning, Lahki, Behl, and Rea said their goodbyes to the village chief and pointed their cart toward their next destination—Branbayna.

Just before nightfall, the party caught sight of a hill next to the road. Atop the hill sat a town surrounded by a stone wall, with tall, box-shaped buildings poking out from inside. From the outside, the town had a dreary feel to it—more like a fort than a place you'd actually want to live. Fields had been carved into the side of the hill, the green of the crops standing out against the surrounding red and brown vista.

Lahki took the cart off the main road and onto a path leading up the hill, arriving at the gate. After greeting the guard and showing him his license as an iron-goods trader under the merchant guild, they were allowed to enter the town.

Lahki drove the cart through the gate while Behl and Rea walked behind him.

Behl let out a yawn. "Haaaaah! We've finally made it to Branbayna. The capital isn't too far off now."

Rea nodded. "Should be another three or four days, yeah?"

Lahki turned the cart toward the inn they'd be staying in. "We already sold off most of the goods we picked up in Luvierte. Now that we have a lighter cart, what do you think about increasing the pace so we can get to the capital quicker?"

His companions both raised their hands in agreement.

Behl laced his fingers behind his head and glanced around the town. "You know, I'm sure seeing a lot more mercenaries around than I remember seeing the last time we were here."

Lahki frowned. "Maybe they're here to deal with

whatever monster chased out the goblins, or some other hunting expedition? We should ask the innkeeper."

After arriving at their usual inn in Branbayna, Lahki parked the cart and handed the horse's reins over to Behl to take it to the stable, then made his way inside to arrange rooms and talk with the innkeeper.

Behl returned just as Lahki was making his way upstairs.

"Hey, Lahki, did you find out what's up?"

Lahki repeated the conversation he'd just had with the innkeeper. "Apparently, there have been many recent sightings of sand wyverns in large groups."

"Huh, makes sense. Leather from sand wyverns is pretty valuable." Behl fell into his role as a bodyguard and began evaluating the danger they could be facing. "I guess that means you'll want to stick around town for a while?"

If a group of wyverns or similar monsters descended upon the cart, there would be little that Behl and Rea on their own could do to stop them.

"Sand wyverns aren't very active during the day, so we should be able to make it to the next town without any problems, as long as we leave before noon."

The serious expression instantly left Behl's face, replaced with an excited grin. He threw his fist up into the air. "Awright, we can sleep in tomorrow!"

"Sure, sure. Anyway, let's go get Rea and head to dinner."

Lahki tried to calm Behl down as they made their way to Rea's room.

The next day, the sun was already high in the sky by the time Lahki steered his cart out of Branbayna and made his way down the road. Black, rocky mountains jutted out from the vast, brown landscape. Behl kept his head constantly moving as he walked next to the cart. Late in the afternoon, he finally spotted something.

From a distance, it looked like a monster lying in wait for its prey, but as they got closer, Behl's expression turned from caution to surprise. "Hey, Lahki, is that a dead sand wyvern over there?"

Lahki looked where Behl was pointing and spotted several of the winged creatures splayed out across the fields. In contrast to their massive wingspan, their bodies were relatively small, looking almost like lizards with birds' heads attached to the ends of their elongated necks. Their dusty yellow skin was covered in a striped pattern. These were definitely sand wyverns, the kind that inhabited the Hibbot wasteland.

They could see at least eight from where they were, none of which bore any obvious injuries. They were just...discarded along the side of the road, in near-perfect condition.

Lahki stopped the cart and looked down. "I think you're right."

Rea cocked her head. "It doesn't look like they've been dead all that long, either."

Behl leaned in for a closer look, a puzzled look on his face as he inspected a hole in the sand wyvern's chest.

"Their rune stones have been taken, which means humans must have done this. But why would they just throw the bodies away? Sand wyvern leather is worth far more than their rune stones."

Lahki hopped down from the driver's seat to look at the sand wyvern's hide. There were a few scorch marks, but it was otherwise in good condition. Judging by the lack of arrow or sword wounds, they must have been killed by magic.

Sand wyvern hides were no stronger than normal wyverns' hides once they were tanned. However, they were much smoother to the touch and harder to procure, making them far more valuable.

In this condition, even the hide from a single sand wyvern would fetch a high price. And any force strong enough to take down so many powerful monsters at once shouldn't have any problem transporting their bodies. No matter how hard he puzzled it over, Lahki couldn't figure out why someone would take the rune stones and leave the rest.

Rea prodded the sand wyvern with her foot. "Well, it'd be a shame to just leave them here. Why don't we take them to the capital and sell them?"

Lahki rubbed his chin. "In this condition, each one should be worth about sixty sok."

Behl's eyes went wide. "Whoa! Sixty gold coins apiece, huh? I wonder how they'd fetch as leather..."

Lahki pulled a large hatchet from the back of his cart. "Let's chop off the excess meat and load 'em in the cart."

"Let me lend you a hand!" Behl was quick to offer his assistance, but Rea just sat down in the bed of the cart.

"I'll stand guard. Good luck with the chopping, you two."

"We'll probably be able to fit three of them in the cart, and that's if we stuff them in..."

Lahki let out a contented sigh. Just thinking about what would be waiting for him in the capital made it impossible for him to keep the excited grin off his face.

Afterword

GREETINGS! This is Ennki Hakari. First off, I can't thank you enough for picking up this second volume of *Skeleton Knight In Another World*. It's thanks to all of my readers that this book got published.

Truly, thank you so much.

I would also like to thank my editor, who had an even tougher time with me on this volume and was constantly pointing out my horrible spelling; my ever-grinning illustrator KeG; and everyone else who helped out. I couldn't have done it without you.

Last time, my afterword ran way too long and we ate into our already-limited page count, so I think I'll keep it short this time to give us a little more room to work with (and so we don't need to make edits down to the individual letter!).

If Arc's story does continue, which is entirely on me, then I want to make the third volume even more polished.

I hope to see you again in the next exciting chapter! Goodbye, and thanks again.

SEPTEMBER 2015—ENNKI HAKARI

Experience these great **light novel** titles from Seven Seas Entertainment